B52 026 741 3
KT-429-813

SPECIAL MESSAGE TO READERS

THE ULVERSCROFT FOUNDATION
(registered UK charity number 264873)
was established in 1972 to provide funds for research, diagnosis and treatment of eye diseases. Examples of major projects funded by the Ulverscroft Foundation are:-

- The Children's Eye Unit at Moorfields Eye Hospital, London
- The Ulverscroft Children's Eye Unit at Great Ormond Street Hospital for Sick Children
- Funding research into eye diseases and treatment at the Department of Ophthalmology, University of Leicester
- The Ulverscroft Vision Research Group, Institute of Child Health
- Twin operating theatres at the Western Ophthalmic Hospital, London
- The Chair of Ophthalmology at the Royal Australian College of Ophthalmologists

You can help further the work of the Foundation by making a donation or leaving a legacy. Every contribution is gratefully received. If you would like to help support the Foundation or require further information, please contact:

THE ULVERSCROFT FOUNDATION
The Green, Bradgate Road, Anstey
Leicester LE7 7FU, England
Tel: (0116) 236 4325

website: www.foundation.ulverscroft.com

WITH LOVE FROM AUNT RUBY

When her engagement to Tom Carson is broken off, Alyssa Grant exchanges city life for an extended stay in the small Canadian town where her elderly Aunt Ruby is recovering from an injury. Ruby, a retired schoolteacher who is determined to set the world to rights, now has a new mission: to help her niece find her way back to happiness. Will Alyssa be reunited with Tom, or find a new love with Ruby's choice, handsome policeman Ben O'Hare?

Books by Catriona McCuaig in the Linford Romance Library:

ICE MAIDEN
MAIL ORDER BRIDE
OUT OF THE SHADOWS
ROMANY ROSE
DOWN LILAC LANE
AT SEAGULL BAY
GHOST WRITER
WHEN THE DAFFODILS BLOOM AGAIN
DARK MOON
TO LOVE AGAIN
IN A WELSH VALLEY
BITTER HARVEST
CHERRY STONES
HEART OF DARKNESS
FOLLOW YOUR HEART
A FAMILY AFFAIR
VICTORIAN SUMMER
HEARTS IN EXILE
PRAIRIE ROSE

CATRIONA McCUAIG

WITH LOVE FROM AUNT RUBY

Complete and Unabridged

LINFORD
Leicester

First published in Great Britain in 2013

First Linford Edition
published 2014

A catalogue record for this book is available from the British Library.

ISBN 978–1–4448–2117–8

Published by
F. A. Thorpe (Publishing)
Anstey, Leicestershire

Set by Words & Graphics Ltd.
Anstey, Leicestershire
Printed and bound in Great Britain by
T. J. International Ltd., Padstow, Cornwall

This book is printed on acid-free paper

1

Alyssa Grant hardly noticed what was going on around her as she stumbled down the tree-lined street. There must have been muted traffic noises, or the twittering of birds in the maples above her head, but she was unaware of them. Her whole world had just come crashing down and she needed time to process what had happened. On reaching home she crept past the side of the house, choosing not to go inside. Steven was probably there, and she couldn't face a barrage of questions right now. Instead, she ran towards the gazebo, planning to sit there until her head cleared.

'Hello! I didn't expect you'd be home yet.' Curses! Her brother was in there, sprawled on a wicker couch, surrounded by papers and books.

'Sorry, I didn't know you were here,'

she muttered, backing away. 'Don't let me interrupt.'

'You're not interrupting. I'm due for a break, anyway. Come on in. I have iced tea.'

Wincing at the word 'break', Alyssa hesitated. *Might as well get it over with,* she told herself. *He'll have to know, sooner or later.*

Ice cubes rattled as Steven poured her a glass of tea from a covered jug. 'So where is Tom? I thought you two had plans to go over to Toronto Island for a picnic.'

'That's all off. In fact, everything is off!'

Steven frowned. 'Off?'

'Yeah. Off. Over. Finito!'

'I don't understand. Are you talking about the wedding? Your engagement? What's going on, for goodness sake?'

Alyssa sank down on the bench. 'I hardly know, Steve. Tom's been acting strangely for days, as if he's brooding over something. Now he tells me he doesn't think he's ready for marriage, so we'd better call the wedding off. He needs to find himself first, whatever that means. He kept muttering something about not knowing who he really is. Honestly, if I didn't know he was only twenty-eight I'd swear he was going through the male menopause.'

'Aren't you being a bit dramatic? The poor guy's probably just having an off day, in a panic at the thought of mortgages and fatherhood in the future, and everything else that goes with marriage. Everyone gets pre-wedding jitters. Give him a couple of days and everything will be fine — you'll see.'

'Not much chance of that!' Alyssa snapped. 'I've given him the ring back. Oh, don't worry; I didn't throw it into Lake Ontario, or anything dramatic like that. Diamonds cost money! No, I was quite reasonable. I said that if the thought of marriage to me dismayed him that much, then of course he mustn't think of going through with it. That's when I pulled the ring off my finger and dropped it into his jacket pocket.'

'Ouch!'

'That's right, side with him, you brute! You men are all the same!'

'Of course I'm on your side, sis. In fact, more than you know.'

'What?'

Steven studied his nails. 'I wasn't going to tell you this, but under the circumstances . . . '

Alyssa frowned. 'You know something, don't you?'

'Well actually, I have seen old Tom out and about with a rather luscious girl lately. Quite a few times, in fact.'

'What?'

'Must you keep saying that? I didn't mention it because I didn't want to make trouble. And for all I knew, she might be his sister. Or sister-in-law.'

'Tom is an only child. I know I've told you that, Steve Grant.'

'I'm a busy man. I can't remember everything I hear you babbling on about.'

'You could if you tried. Tell me about this girl, then. I'm sure it's something quite innocent, like she stopped him to ask for directions, perhaps.'

'Medium height, a figure that goes in and out in all the right places, and dark hair that always looks like it's just been shampooed,' Steven rhymed off in typical bachelor style. 'I didn't get close enough to see the colour of her eyes. There, is that good enough for you?'

'But what were they doing?'

'Well, one evening they were going into the Rialto, where the latest James Bond is playing. Remind me to go and see that, Alyssa. I've heard it's a good one.'

'Steven!'

'Yes, well, a couple of times I've seen them eating in one of those outdoor cafes; not my idea of a good meal, with all the traffic dust blowing in on you from the street. Other than that, I've just seen them walking down the street together. Arm in arm.' He cleared his throat, looking up at her uncertainly.

'That's it, then!' Alyssa replied, thumping her fist on the table. 'He's found somebody else, and not content with cheating on me he's lied, too, making half-baked excuses as if I'm a nitwit who'd swallow anything he'd throw at me. Well! It looks like I've had a narrow escape. Thank goodness I found out in time!' She burst into tears and rushed out of the gazebo.

There was only one thing to do. An hour's nap, cowering under the duvet, would go a long way towards putting her right, and perhaps when she woke up again she'd find that it had all been a dream, or at least a mere blip on her radar. Tom would be all apologies, perhaps saying that a bit of trouble at work had thrown him off base, and in no time at all they'd be back on track.

However the phone didn't ring once, and Alyssa awoke to find that it was past four o'clock, she'd missed lunch, and that Tom apparently couldn't care less about her feelings. She sat up suddenly. Wait a minute! In view of the way they'd parted he might be afraid to phone in case she hung up on him. Email would be a better bet. She could imagine him deciding that she might at least glance over it before deleting the thing.

But that thought evidently hadn't occurred to Tom, for the only message on Alyssa's iMac was from her mother in Australia. It was full of chatty news about places and people that she'd never heard of. 'And we really must firm up the arrangements for the wedding very soon,' Anna Grant had written. 'If we want to book the golf club for the reception we'll need to act fast. It's a very popular venue for weddings, or so I'm told. And does Steven intend to come? If so, he'll have to find someone for Pookie and Rybena. Do make sure he does something about that, Alyssa, and soon.'

Alyssa's parents, Greg and Anna Grant, had taken early retirement from their jobs and were now living their dream of travelling the world. Well, not exactly the whole world; just making extended stays in the countries they most wanted to visit. That excluded any place where they might get mauled by tigers, swept away in giant mudslides or forced to tangle with enormous creepy-crawlies. They had spent an enchanted year in Ireland — that was safe enough as far as Anna was concerned, because St Patrick had driven out all the snakes, she had asserted — and now they were in Australia, staying near the home of some distant cousins.

The master plan was that Alyssa and Tom would get married there, in a Christmas wedding with a difference. It would be summer Down Under and they could have their reception on the beach: the wedding, too, if they so chose. Alyssa had never dreamed of a huge church wedding, followed by a reception catering to hundreds of people, most of whom she hardly knew. Nor did she relish spending a thousand dollars on a gown that would be worn once. Some people wanted those things, and more power to them if they could afford it, but that was not her style. Her savings would be spent on the airfare to Australia, and the romantic honeymoon that followed.

She wiped away a tear. She desperately wanted to go and look for Tom. She wanted to throw her arms around him and she needed to hear him say that it had all been a mistake. But she must remember the dark-haired beauty. If Tom had fallen in love with that other girl, then let him get on with it. Alyssa was too proud to beg.

2

'I'm just going for a Chinese meal,' Steven called up the stairs. 'Do you want to come? You'll have to if you want to eat tonight. There's nothing in the fridge. Or shall I bring back a takeout?'

'Give me five minutes,' Alyssa shouted. Rats! She'd promised to do a big shop on the way home from the picnic, but her break-up with Tom had put all thoughts of that out of her head. Hastily, she washed her face, pulled on a clean T-shirt and ran a comb through her auburn curls. Grabbing her purse, she ran down to join her brother.

The subdued lighting and the familiar surroundings at the Golden Dragon went a long way towards calming Alyssa's shattered nerves. Although she'd been dining here for years, she had never come here with Tom because, for some reason, he detested Chinese food. As they had always done, she and Steven ordered chicken fried rice plus one favouite dish each, which would be shared between them. Alyssa selected sweet-and-sour chicken balls while her brother dithered between spare ribs and chicken chow mein.

'No veggies?' she teased, when he finally settled on the spare ribs, as she'd known he would.

'I can get veggies any time,' he retorted. 'Besides, there's cabbage in the egg rolls.'

When the young waitress had departed, taking the enormous menus with her, Steven cleared his throat. 'Have you heard from Tom?'

'No, I have not. And I don't want to, either!'

'Come on, sis, you don't mean that.'

She dabbed at her eyes with the corner of her magenta-coloured napkin. 'How could he treat me like this, Steve? You tell me that! We were going to be married, for goodness sake! But to judge by what you've seen, this thing with the raven-haired beauty must have been going on for some time. I'm just so hurt by all this, and how I'm going to tell Mum I don't know. She's just sent me an email wanting me to firm up her plans for the wedding.'

'Never mind Mum. She'll be all sympathy. The question is, what are you going to do next?'

Alyssa spread her hands wide. 'That's a question, all right. I've burned too many bridges because of this so-called wedding. I haven't renewed my contract with the school board, so I'll be out of a job come September. I've let my apartment go, and I'll never find anything else I can afford in Toronto, so I'm homeless. How's that for starters?'

'You're hardly homeless, Lys. You can stay at Mum and Dad's until you sort something out, and you know it.'

'All right for you,' she mumbled, but any further talk was cut off by the return of the waitress carrying a tray piled high with food.

Steven Grant was staying in the flat above his parents' garage, living rent-free in return for looking after their home and pets while they were abroad. Pookie, their mixed-breed dog, was low-maintenance, happy to get his meals and three walks a day; while Rybena, their long-haired white cat, prowled around the house, gazing out of each window in turn. There was too much traffic on the streets for her to be allowed outside, but she seemed contented enough with her restricted lifestyle.

The arrangement suited Steven very well, for he was studying for his bar exams and was happy to be relieved of the need to work at some low-paid job to support himself in the meantime. As for the Grants, this gave them peace of mind, knowing that all was well at home.

'Why not stay on for a while, until you get your head together? It would be a help for me, having someone to share the work,' he said now.

Alyssa threw a packet of soy sauce at him, hitting him on the chin. She knew he wasn't referring to his legal studies. She'd get stuck with the cooking and the laundry while he did the pleasant bits, like mowing the lawn and walking the dog. And staying on in her childhood home held a certain attraction. Wrapped in security and happy memories, she could retreat from the world until she regained her equilibrium.

Their family home was in Mississauga, a suburb of Toronto. Now a city in its own right, overflowing with modern town houses and other expensive dwellings, it was originally a rural area encompassing several small communities. The Grants' large, detached brick house, standing in a quarter of an acre of land, dated from those early days. To buy a modern property of a similar size and acreage would probably cost millions. In fact, Greg Grant had already received offers from property developers, although so far he had resisted all comers.

Although Alyssa had been away from home for several years, teaching school in Toronto, her old bedroom remained as she had left it — right down to Travis, her teddy bear, sitting on her pillow. Yes, it would be good to take a step back into those happy childhood years.

'I can't do it!' she announced at last.

'What can't you do? If you mean you're not going to finish that fried rice, I'll relieve you of it.' Steven reached for the plate, wincing when she rapped him on the knuckles with her spoon.

'I can't just let everything go while my whole life crumbles around me. That would mean that Tom Carson and the witch have won. I'll have to look for a job, for starters.'

'Can't you ring the school board? Tell them your plans have changed?'

'They'll have settled everything for the coming year by now. Of course I could register as a supply teacher, but that's not the easiest job in the world.

You never know what your income is going to be from one month to the next, and of course the kids always play up when faced with a teacher they don't know. Then there's the driving. You have to go where you're sent, which could mean going to the other side of the region in the middle of a snowstorm. Not for me, thanks!'

'I know — why not go out to Australia and stay with Mum and Dad? I know they'd love to see you, and you do have the price of the fare.'

'So I do,' Alyssa said. She'd saved up for months for that. Giving up her daily latte and other small treats had seemed a small price to pay when she'd known that the end result would be a wedding in faraway Australia, heading into the future with the man of her dreams.

'I might,' she murmured, snapping her fortune cookie apart. The message on the tiny slip of paper told her, 'You are going on a journey.' It seemed prophetic, but did it mean a physical journey, or a life change? No matter; it was only a bit of fun.

Her mobile phone vibrated. Hope welled up inside her, only to be crushed a moment later as she took in the fact that Tom wasn't the sender, but Beegrove General Hospital. Who on earth was calling her from there? It must be a wrong number. Disappointed, she stuffed the phone back into her purse.

Something nagged at her as she strolled home with Steven. Great Aunt Ruby lived at Beegrove, but Alyssa had never been there. Beegrove, population five thousand, was a town in Eastern Ontario. As was the case with many Canadian communities, it had been named after the physical attributes discovered by the first settlers, in this case a grove of bees. Years later the town fathers had decided that the name Bee Grove was too rustic for an up-and-coming place.

Beegrove Hospital. Had something happened to Aunt Ruby? And how had they got the number of her mobile phone?

'Only one way to find out,' Steven said. 'Call them back. Unless you'd like me to do it.'

'No, I'd better do it myself. After all, they've got my name from somewhere, so it must be me they want.'

* * *

After a frustrating wait while she selected numbers from a phone menu at the hospital, first having been told that if this was an emergency she should dial 911, Alyssa finally got through to a live person.

'Beegrove General Hospital, Admissions. How may I help you?'

'Um, I don't know if you can. Someone from there seems to have called me earlier.'

'Your name, please?'

'Alyssa Grant.'

'And who is it you wish to speak to?'

'I really have no idea.'

'Are you waiting to hear about a clinic appointment, perhaps?'

'No, no. I'm calling from Mississauga.'

'Then is there a friend or a loved one in this hospital as a patient?'

'As I said, I have no idea. I do have an aunt who lives in Beegrove. Could something have happened to her?'

'Her name, please?'

'Watson. Mrs Ruby Watson.'

'One moment, please, while I check the computer.'

The voice returned. 'Yes, Mrs Ruby Watson was admitted two days ago, after an accident.'

Alyssa gasped. 'What happened to her? Is she all right? She's not dead, is she?'

'I'm afraid I can't release any details, ma'am. Patient confidentiality, you know.'

Alyssa's patience suddenly ran out. 'Look here — this call is costing me money! I've contacted you because I saw the hospital's name on my phone, but I insist on knowing what is going on. There must have been a reason for the hospital to get in touch!'

'Hold the line, please. I'll put you through to the nurses' station on the second floor.'

'At last!' Alyssa found herself speaking to a much more efficient person, who identified herself as the head nurse.

'Yes, we do have your aunt here,' the woman told her when they had gone through the usual preliminaries. 'Mrs Watson has a broken arm and she's recovering from a mild concussion, but she's due to be discharged soon, if suitable arrangements can be made for her.'

'What sort of arrangements? How can I help?'

'That's why we've been trying to get in touch. Mrs Watson has listed her nephew, Mr Gregory Grant, as her next of kin, but I understand that he has referred us to you because he is currently out of the country.'

'Yes, that's my father. My parents are in Australia at the moment and there's nobody else, apart from my brother and myself.'

'In the case of elderly patients — Mrs Watson is eighty-three — our discharge team likes to meet with family members to make sure that everything goes well after they leave the hospital.'

'Discharge team?'

'Yes. That includes her doctor, together with the nurse assigned in that role, and the dietician, and so on. They can assess what resources will be needed to look after the patient in her own home or whether temporary or permanent nursing home care is a more viable option. Are you able to be present, Ms Grant, or should we proceed without you?'

'I'll drive up first thing tomorrow. I should be there in five hours or so, traffic permitting.'

'Good. I look forward to meeting you. Goodbye.'

At least she didn't order me to have a

nice day, Alyssa thought. The popular form of dismissal, beloved of shop assistants and dentists' receptionists alike, always grated on her. In cowardly fashion she always countered this with a smiling, 'You, too!' But one of these days she was going to explode, and the result would not be pretty.

'You're going to drive all the way up there tomorrow?' Steven asked, frowning. 'Do you want me to come with you? I could always bring my books along and study in the car.'

'No, I can manage, thanks.'

'We haven't ever met Great Aunt Ruby, have we? At least, if we have, I must have been pretty small at the time.'

'I don't think so, no. Perhaps it's time we did. The nurse tells me the old girl is eighty-three. Even if she comes through this little bout, she won't live forever.'

'I suppose not. Does she not have any family of her own?'

Alyssa racked her brains in an effort to recall what she knew of Ruby

Watson. 'I guess she doesn't, if we've been listed as next of kin. I know she's a widow, of course. Perhaps I'll email Mum for more details before I go to bed.'

'Good idea. Is there any chance of you making me a grilled cheese sandwich before you go and do it? I feel in need of a little something.'

'Make it yourself, Steven Grant. Although how you can be hungry after that meal you've just eaten beats me!'

'It's always like that with Chinese food. Your stomach swells up or something while you're eating it, and then it settles down and you need something else to keep you going.'

Laughing, Alyssa went to write to her mother. But when morning came and she checked her computer one last time, she still hadn't heard back. Either her parents were away on one of their side trips and were enjoying themselves too much to bother with emails, or it was something to do with the time difference between Canada and Australia. Alyssa still had not managed to work that out, largely because Canada fell into several different time zones.

The temperature climbed as she drove north, making her thankful that her Chevrolet was equipped with air conditioning. Once she was off the crowded motorways she followed a scenic route on lesser highways, passing through small towns and picturesque villages. She stopped for coffee twice, deliberately choosing small restaurants rather than the drive-thru at the ever-present Tim Horton's coffee shops, in order to stretch and rest her shoulders.

Shortly after one o'clock she saw the green sign she'd been watching for: Welcome to Beegrove. Population 5031.

3

Alyssa found her great aunt in a hospital ward containing four beds. The old lady was sitting up in bed reading a copy of *The People's Friend.* Other magazines were scattered about on the green cotton coverlet. She looked up as Alyssa approached.

'Oh, no! Not more tests, please! I'm beginning to feel like a pincushion.'

'Auntie Ruby? I'm Alyssa, Greg's daughter.'

Mrs Watson brightened at once. 'So here you are! I was wondering if they'd manage to get hold of you, dear. Such a nuisance, your father off gallivanting in Australia, of all places! I need him here to do battle with those doctors. Young whippersnappers! No older than you, by the look of things.'

'Never mind,' Alyssa murmured, when at last she managed to get a word in. 'Perhaps I can help. What seems to be the problem?'

'They want to have me put away, dear. Oh, I don't mean an asylum, or whatever they call such places nowadays. But they mean to put me in a home of some sort, and I won't have it! I have my own home, and I plan to stay in it until the bitter end. You'll help me fight them, won't you, dear?'

'Of course I'll do everything I can, Auntie. How are you feeling, anyway? What exactly have you done to yourself?'

'Well, there's this silly old hand,' Ruby replied, indicating the plaster cast on her right arm. 'And apparently I gave myself a whack on the head, although the bump is going down nicely now. If the ladder hadn't rocked I wouldn't have lost my balance, and none of this would have happened.'

'What ladder?' Alyssa was horrified. 'What on earth were you doing up a ladder, Auntie?'

Ruby grinned. 'Thank you for not

adding 'at your age' like the rest of them. There was a hornets' nest under the eave — still there, I expect — and I just wanted to give it a spray to get rid of the little devils. I think I overbalanced when I raised my right arm to give them a blast from the can, and now look at me!'

'Yes, indeed. But surely it wouldn't cost much to pay some neighbour to do that sort of thing for you? A teenager, perhaps, or somebody out of work?'

'Huh! Just you try it. Either they promise to come and never show up, or they wander off in the middle of a job and are never seen again. Been there, done that, bought the T-shirt!'

Alyssa tried to hide a smile. 'I suppose I'd better go and have a word with the head nurse to find out when this conference of yours is scheduled.'

'If you can find her. All these young nurses are decked out in floral tops and pants and a body can't tell whether they're visitors, nurses or cleaning women. In my day nurses wore starched white dresses and caps. You knew where you were then.'

Alyssa decided that this was still very much Ruby Watson's day. Clearly the lady had 'all her marbles', as Dad would say.

'And if you hand me my purse — it's in the bedside table there — I'll give you my house key. I suppose you can find your way to my place if I give you directions? Make yourself at home, dear, and I'll see you tomorrow.'

The following day Alyssa found herself in a small meeting room at the hospital, furnished with several soft armchairs and tastefully decorated with framed landscapes on the wall. A young doctor was perched on the edge of a table, swinging his legs, and several women reclined in the chairs nearby. As Aunt Ruby had said, it was impossible to know their status, although each wore a nametag complete with photograph. A near-sighted patient would not glean any understanding from those. Aunt Ruby herself sat in a wheelchair, glowering.

'Before you start,' she announced, 'I am not leaving my home, so that's it. Case closed!'

'We're just looking for a temporary solution, Mrs Watson,' the head nurse told her. 'It's quite obvious that you can't manage alone, with your right arm out of commission. We'll be able to supply you with a home care worker for a short period each day, to do light housework and assist you to wash and dress, but at this stage you need something more.' She turned to Alyssa. 'How long are you planning to stay, Ms Grant?'

'You can leave her out of it!' Ruby snapped — rather ungratefully, Alyssa thought, considering the fact that she'd raced up here at the drop of a hat, all the way from Mississauga.

The doctor spoke for the first time. 'Perhaps we could get you into Partridge Run for a few weeks.' He turned to Alyssa. 'That's our local retirement centre. Residents have their own rooms there with a communal dining room and lounge. Part of the complex is reserved for short-term stays by otherwise healthy people who need extra help while recovering from accidents or surgery. Wouldn't you enjoy that, Mrs Watson?'

'It sounds lovely, apart from the ridiculous name, but where would I get the money? My friend Martha spent a month in there after she had her varicose veins done, and it cost her two thousand dollars a week. A week!'

'Do you not have something put by for a rainy day, Mrs Watson?'

'Certainly I do, but if I dip into that it's gone, and where will I be the next time something goes wrong?'

Frustrated, the doctor outlined other options, all of which Ruby steadfastly refused. She didn't want to sell her home and move to what she called 'an old folks' apartment', nor was she ready to enter the 'old folks' home'.

This was getting them nowhere. When the doctor sighed and said that the only other alternative was to transfer her to the third floor of the hospital, where the chronically ill were kept in limbo, Alyssa came to life. She surprised herself by announcing that Aunt Ruby would be able to stay in her own home because she, Alyssa, would temporarily move in to take care of her.

There were relieved smiles all round but Ruby said nothing until she was back in bed. Then she whispered her thanks. 'I didn't say anything back there because I'm determined to get out of here, by fair means or foul!'

'Is it really that bad in here, Auntie?'

'Oh, they've all been very kind, dear, but I can't wait to get a decent cup of tea. Do you know, they bring you a tea bag and a pot of lukewarm water, and they expect you to make do with that. Ugh!'

'Ugh indeed!' Alyssa, who liked her tea scalding hot, could certainly emphasise with that.

'I do understand that you can't stay,' Ruby went on. 'Never mind, I'll manage somehow.'

'Oh, but I meant it, Auntie. I can stay for as long as you need me.'

'But your job. Don't you have to go back to school eventually? And I understood from your mother's last letter that you're engaged to be married. Surely you have wedding plans to make?'

'Oh, that's all off, I'm afraid. And as for the job, that's gone as well. So you see, I'm free as a bird, and there is absolutely no need for you to go into the Hen Coop or whatever they call it, even if you could manage to scrape the money together.'

'I see. Well, you can tell me all about it later. Meanwhile, I think we should get out of here before that young doctor changes his mind about letting me go. If you can help me back into that beastly wheelchair we'll go and check out. You'll have to sign the discharge papers for me. I never was very good at writing with my left hand.'

After a certain amount of huffing and

puffing, Aunt Ruby was installed in Alyssa's car, and they set off for home, an old-fashioned brick house on a quiet street.

'It's a bit big for one person,' Ruby explained when they were sitting in her airy kitchen, waiting for the kettle to boil, 'but it's home and I can't imagine living anywhere else. I hope you'll enjoy your stay here, dear. I've been after your parents for years to bring you and your little brother to stay with me, but it hasn't happened until now.'

'Not so little any more, Auntie. Steven is studying for his bar exams now.'

'Fancy!'

* * *

Upstairs in the spare bedroom — 'You'll need to flick a duster around the place before you settle in, dear' — Alyssa unpacked the few clothes she'd brought with her, wondering if she was doing the right thing. Mississauga seemed so far away, and Tom a distant and painful memory. However, this enforced absence would afford her some breathing space while she tried to decide on her next move, and that could only be a good thing.

4

'You must think I'm a miserable old grouch,' Aunt Ruby said with a wry smile. 'Shooting down every suggestion those poor young people made. The thing is, when you're eighty-three years old people tend to think they know what's best for you, and it's their job to parcel you up and ship you in the right direction. That's all very well for someone who's infirm or incapable, but I'm not senile yet. Far from it! I may have broken a bone, but there's nothing wrong with my head.'

'Of course not,' Alyssa murmured.

'Mind you, I don't know if I'd have got away with it so easily if you hadn't been there, my dear, and I'm grateful. I do understand, however, that you haven't signed on for the next few months. We'll need to put our heads together and make a plan for what to do when you go back to Mississauga.'

'No need to worry about that, Auntie; I'm here for the duration.'

'Oh? How do you make that out, then? I hope you're not contemplating postponing your wedding because of me, child, for I won't hear of it.'

'As I've told you, the wedding is off. And before you tell me I should go to Tom and say I've changed my mind, I must point out that he was the one with cold feet, not me.'

'And did he say why?'

'Oh, he spouted some rigmarole about needing to find himself, but that was all a lie. Tom didn't even have the grace to tell me the truth. Steven has seen him several times, out with the same girl, looking very chummy indeed. Hard though it might be, I could understand it if he'd fallen for somebody else in all innocence — but he might at least have explained that to me. Surely he owes me that, after all we've meant to each other?'

'One would certainly think so.

Perhaps he'll think better of it in time, and let you know what's bothering him. But your Thomas aside; don't you have to go back to school in September?'

Alyssa shrugged. 'And that's another thing. I didn't renew my contract because I thought I was going to Australia, so I'm out of work as well.'

'I'm sorry to hear that, dear.'

'I'm not sorry, as it happens, although being jobless is a worry. Teaching isn't what it used to be. Somehow the children seem to have gained the upper hand. If a child simply won't obey there is very little the teacher can do without the parents rushing to the school to complain. And if you send the child to the principal as a last resort, she can't do much, either, without bringing the wrath of the parents down on her head, howling because we've affected their little darling's self-esteem.'

'Perhaps you should apply for a job here, Alyssa. We don't seem to suffer as much from that sort of nonsense here, being in a small town.'

'I suppose it was all different in your day, eh? When you had to walk ten miles to school, uphill all the way, according to Dad, you were too exhausted to play up in class!'

'Cheeky!' Ruby's eyes twinkled in response to Alyssa's little joke. 'Mind you, when I was young you got the strap if you misbehaved, and if you complained about it when you got home your parents wanted to know what you'd done to deserve it, and often you got another dose! As perhaps you know, I went through training to be a teacher when I left school; we attended what was known as Normal School for a year before being sent out to a one-room schoolhouse in the country, teaching all eight grades at once.'

'Only a year!' Alyssa marvelled. Her year of teacher training at university had followed a basic three-year degree. She wondered how on earth the women of Aunt Ruby's generation had managed on a mere year of post-secondary education.

'Of course we had to keep taking summer courses and night classes after that,' Ruby went on, perhaps divining what was going through her great-niece's mind. 'I had to stop teaching when I married Philip, of course. Married women didn't teach in those days. Later, when the rules changed, I returned to the profession, teaching grade four in Beegrove Elementary. Happy days!'

'You must miss it.'

'Not really. After all, I've been retired since 1994. Mind you, they do call me in occasionally, especially on Heritage Day, to talk about what the kiddies call the olden days. They seem really interested when I show them some of our games — hopscotch, skipping and the like — but as far as I know, they forget all about it after I leave. When did you last see little girls playing with a skipping rope, Alyssa, chanting rhymes as they waited for their turn? House to let, apply within, the people upstairs are drinking gin . . . '

'I don't think I've heard that one,' Alyssa laughed. 'I don't suppose the nanny state would allow that on school grounds today.'

'Ah, well, that's life. Everything changes. There's just one thing I can't stand, though. It's hearing a perfectly healthy child complaining of boredom. In my day we'd have been told to find something constructive to do, or something would be found for us, and we wouldn't like what that was!'

Alyssa smiled again. Older people did tend to ramble on, convinced that everything had been better in their day. Never mind; it was good for Aunt Ruby to have her say, and very interesting it was, too. Alyssa toyed with the idea of writing down some of her great-aunt's memories, to share with the rest of the family at a later date.

What she had no way of knowing was that Ruby was busy formulating a plan that would not only fill in the time while she was recuperating from her fall, but benefit the community while she was at it. And, as a welcome side effect, these activities would influence her niece's future love life as well.

* * *

A week had gone by, during which Alyssa had shopped for groceries, taken a walking tour of Beegrove, and driven Aunt Ruby to her Women's Institute meeting. There had been no word from Tom, and according to Steven her ex-fiancé seemed to have vanished off the face of the earth.

'I went round to his place but it's all locked up, and his next-door neighbour thinks he's gone to Australia,' Steven said in an email. 'She's behind the times, of course, but I didn't contradict her. The less everyone knows, the better, eh?'

* * *

The email from their mother was longer, and full of questions that Alyssa couldn't answer. She was shocked to realise that only a few days ago she'd been planning to adopt Steven's suggestion and fly out to Australia, to wallow in the sympathy of her concerned parents. Now she'd changed direction completely and was becoming immersed in the life of Beegrove, Ontario. Determined not to let her parents know the depth of her hurt, she filled her letters with cheery messages about Aunt Ruby's progress and all their doings.

The first intimation of the older lady's plan came when she visited her doctor for a check-up. Alyssa accompanied her to the doctor's office, which was set in a large brick house, formerly a private home in the days when people had large families. It had been remodelled to accommodate a large waiting room and a number of consulting rooms on the ground floor. An archway at one end of the waiting room gave access to an alcove where a receptionist worked behind a counter. A nurse in a white pantsuit and trainers appeared from time to time; apparently the hospital's modern dress code hadn't yet penetrated here, although the woman did not wear the cap of her hospital training school.

A small boy sat on the floor near a box of battered toys, moving a car about to the accompaniment of ear-splitting *vroom-vroom* noises. Ruby watched him, her expression grim, but she said nothing and the child's mother appeared not to notice.

'Mrs Hamilton?' The nurse had reappeared. 'Doctor Mason will see you now.' Alyssa hadn't seen anyone leaving, so perhaps there was a separate exit.

'Now you behave yourself, Jason. Mommy won't be long, and she'll get you a Happy Meal on the way home if you're a good boy.'

By way of reply, Jason took his shrieks up a few decibels. Alyssa clapped her hands over her ears. Moments later the child scrambled up on the chair vacated by his mother, fixing Aunt Ruby with a gimlet eye. 'I'm bored!' he announced. Aunt Ruby smiled sweetly.

'Are you, dear? Well, there's good news. Dr Mason can fix that for you.'

'Huh?'

'Oh, yes. She can give you a needle for that and you'll never feel bored again. It's a great big syringe' — here Ruby held up her left hand, with thumb and index finger spread wide — 'but you'll feel so much better when it's all over. When Mommy comes back we'll ask her to get one for you, shall we?'

After a moment of appalled silence, the child opened his mouth wide in a loud roar of indignation that brought all eyes in their direction. Alyssa hardly knew where to look. For her part, Aunt Ruby was the picture of innocence, smiling and shrugging as if to imply that the child's outburst was unwarranted and unexpected. The receptionist hastened out from behind her counter, clutching a small green lollipop.

'I don't feel well,' Ruby told her, clutching her heart. 'If you don't mind I'll go home now.'

'Would you like a glass of water?'

'No, thank you. I'll be all right once I get out in the fresh air. My niece will call you later to reschedule my appointment.'

'Chicken!' Alyssa muttered.

'What was that, Miss?'

'Stricken. I said that my aunt is stricken with nerves when there's too much noise. Older people are like that, aren't they?

'How could you?' Alyssa demanded when they were back in her car, buckling their seat belts. 'Frightening that poor child half to death like that!'

'He needed sorting out, sneering at me like that. Bored, indeed! Well, I bet he won't say that again in a hurry. And it worked, didn't it? He got the attention he was looking for, and a lollipop as well.'

'But he probably believed you, and now he'll be fearful the next time he has to have a necessary vaccination. It's a good thing his mother didn't hear what you were up to.'

'Why do you think I beat a hasty retreat, my girl? Next time I'll be better prepared, you'll see.'

5

Alyssa emailed her brother again. She had to know what was going on with Tom.

'I told you, Lys! I haven't seen hide nor hair of the guy. Anyway, it's up to you to sort this out, surely? Call him, for heaven's sake! Insist on having an explanation! Don't be a womouse.'

Alyssa stared at the screen of her laptop. This was an old joke between them, Steven insisting that there had to be a feminine version of the question 'are you a man or a mouse?' As he put it, 'Are you a woman or a womouse?'

'I am a womouse, aren't I?' she said aloud, just as Aunt Ruby came into the room.

'What was that, dear?'

'Oh, nothing, Auntie. I was just thinking out loud.'

'It didn't sound like nothing to me.

You're still fretting over that Thomas of yours, I suppose.'

'Are far as I'm concerned, Tom Carson can go and drown himself in Lake Ontario!'

'Come now, dear, I know you don't mean that.'

'Well, of course I don't wish him any harm, but I hate the way he's treated me. I haven't *done* anything, Auntie! As far as I knew everything was right on target: Australia, the wedding, everything! It's not just that he lied to me, you know. Let's leave the other girl out of it for a moment. Say he really did have second thoughts about marrying me. That couldn't have come over him all of a sudden. Surely his doubts would have come on gradually?'

'So what are you saying?'

'I've given up my job and my apartment, all because we were soon to go to Australia. He was well aware of that, and he must have realised how it would all impact on me, so why not say something sooner? Now I'm jobless and homeless and my wedding is off. What on earth is the matter with him?' Alyssa fumbled in her pocket for a tissue.

Aunt Ruby sat down, looking stern. 'Well of course if it's a pity party you want, we can sit here and wallow in it all day. I'm not going anywhere and I do so enjoy a good moan.'

Alyssa stared at her, shocked. 'Auntie! You don't sound very sympathetic!'

'It's not sympathy you need, my girl. It's a bit of backbone! Go and see this Thomas and insist he tells you what's really on his mind. Perhaps he's had second thoughts by now, and you'll be able to take it from there.'

'I've already thought of that but I can't seem to reach him. My emails bounce back and when I try him on his mobile it just goes to voice mail. Steven has tried to locate him but he seems to have disappeared off the face of the earth.'

'Then here's what I suggest you do. Write him a letter the old-fashioned way, sent by Canada Post. Give him an ultimatum. If you haven't heard back from him by a certain date — say a month from now — you intend to move forward with your plans for a life without him.'

'Plans! Don't I wish!'

'Don't sound so bitter, dear. It doesn't become you. Why not go out to your parents in Australia? A change of scene would do you good.'

Alyssa shook her head. 'That would only make me feel worse, considering the fact that we'd meant to go out there together for our wedding.'

'Then you must proceed to Plan B.'

'And what's that? Go to a convent?'

'You can stay here with me. This house is too big for one person, in any case. Pay me rent if it makes you feel any better.'

'I'd love to stay here with you, Auntie, but you're forgetting one thing. I must find a job, and it's too late to find a teaching post for this year.'

'Who says it has to be a teaching job? Try Tim Horton's, or the supermarket.

Or register for supply teaching, and do volunteer work on the side.'

Alyssa shook her head in amazement. 'You've got it all figured out, haven't you?'

Ruby smiled. 'I know you think I'm a bit dotty, dear — oh, don't deny it; I could see how embarrassed you were at the doctor's office — but I'm not a needy old bird. When your uncle Philip died there's no denying I was knocked for a loop for a while, but I soon realised that if I was to carry on alone here I'd have to take charge of my own affairs. It took me a while to get my priorities straight, but that's a story for another day. Suffice to say that I managed to sort myself out, and that's why I'm the woman I am today. Now then, I think a cup of tea is called for, don't you?'

'Let me make it,' Alyssa insisted, jumping to her feet.

* * *

Two days later Alssa was sitting at the kitchen table with her laptop in front of her, trying to draft that letter to Tom. Aunt Ruby had gone out to return her library book, brushing aside Alyssa's offer to drive her there.

'The library isn't far away — just at the other end of Main Street — and the walk will do me good. I've got the book in my backpack, if you'll kindly help me on with it. Now hand me my cane, please, and I'll be on my way.'

Alyssa reached for the sturdy walking stick with its handle shaped like the head of a Labrador retriever, and passed it to her aunt. 'If you don't feel up to walking back, get the librarian to give me a call and I'll drive over to pick you up.'

'Nonsense! It's my wrist that's broken, not my leg. How old do you think I am, ninety?'

Laughing, Alyssa closed the door behind the feisty old lady and went to boot up her computer.

When the kitchen phone extension rang half an hour later, she decided that Ruby needed her after all. Expecting to hear the dulcet tones of Miss Phipps at the library, she was puzzled to hear a man's voice on a crackling line. Concluding that it was probably a telemarketer, she was about to hang up when the man spoke again.

'Hello? Is that Ms Grant?'

'Yes, it is. Who is speaking, please?'

'This is Constable Benjamin O'Hare, calling from the police station. It's about Mrs Watson. I'm afraid there's been an accident.'

'Oh, no! Is she all right? I mean, she isn't . . . '

'No, no, nothing like that. She's just a bit shaken, that's all, but she can't be released until we know she'll be taken care of.'

'Is she at the hospital?'

'No, she's here at the police station. I'll explain everything when you come.'

* * *

'It took you long enough to get here, my girl!' Aunt Ruby was seated in a swivel chair, with a Tim Horton's coffee cup in her left hand. Alyssa could see that the old lady was annoyed.

'I'm so sorry, Auntie! I was a bit flustered after Constable O'Hare called and I had trouble finding this place. What happened to you? You weren't struck by a car or anything, were you?'

'Ms Grant? I'm glad you could come. I'm Ben O'Hare.'

Alyssa swung round at the sound of his voice. Well, he was certainly a sight for sore eyes. He was six feet tall, trim and muscular in his navy blue uniform, with unruly red hair and tawny eyes. 'How do you do?' she said.

'Well, I've had better days, ma'am. I'm afraid your aunt is in a bit of trouble.'

'Nonsense!' Aunt Ruby chipped in. 'I'm the innocent bystander here. I'm the one who was flat on the sidewalk. I could have broken my hip, and you know what that means, at my age!

Weeks in hospital, and lucky if I didn't get pneumonia and pop off as a result!'

'But what happened, Auntie?'

'I was on my way to the library, just minding my own business, when this young hooligan came speeding along on a bicycle and knocked me off my feet. It's quite illegal for cyclists to use the sidewalk instead of the street.'

O'Hare folded his arms. 'That's not quite the whole story, is it, Mrs Watson? Why don't you tell us the rest?'

Aunt Ruby blushed. 'I did say something to him as he shot past, doing those wheelie things they get up to. He actually turned round and shouted, 'Get lost, grandma!' The nerve of the child! It quite took my breath away for a few minutes, I can tell you!'

'Go on, ma'am,' O'Hare prompted. 'Tell us the rest.'

'Well, when he reached the end of the street he turned round and came racing back still on the sidewalk. I held my cane out to steady myself and somehow it got tangled up with his wheel and the pair of us fell to the ground. Mr Glover saw it all. He came out of the menswear shop and helped me up. His assistant took the child by the ear and took him inside, while we waited for the Law to come.'

'And that was a mistake, too,' O'Hare grumbled. 'Laying hands on the boy like that. The parents could have him in court for assault.'

'Then I hope they do, for I'll be more than happy to stand up and tell the judge what really happened. And you can just tell that child's parents that I expect a written apology from that little horror. He can't grow up thinking he can run down elderly ladies without paying the price.'

'Perhaps we should just let well enough alone, Mrs Watson, eh?'

Alyssa stared at the constable in surprise. Perhaps the child's misdemeanour wasn't worthy of a court appearance and subsequent juvenile crime record, but surely he shouldn't get off scot-free?

'Can my aunt leave now, constable? I really think we should go the emergency room just to make sure she's all right.'

'Not today, thank you,' Ruby piped up. 'I have no wish to sit there for four hours surrounded by chatty old men and children with runny noses, waiting to be seen by some overworked doctor who will only tell me to take two aspirin and see my own doctor if I start frothing at the mouth. I never did get to the library, so we'll drive there now, and then we'll go home and take that aspirin. As for you, Benjy O'Hare, I'll leave it to you to make sure that little monster gets his just deserts. Come along, Alyssa!'

'Benjy?' Alyssa asked, when she was leaning over to fasten her aunt's seat belt. 'Did he say you could call him that?'

Aunt Ruby grinned. 'I was his kindergarten teacher, child. I've known that lad since the day he was born.'

Alyssa hesitated. 'Just tell me one thing,

Auntie. It was a genuine accident, wasn't it? You didn't stick your cane through his spokes on purpose, did you?'

Aunt Ruby looked her full in the eye, her expression bland. 'Now why would I do a thing like that?'

'Well, he was riding on the sidewalk, where he shouldn't have been. He was rude to you. Then he deliberately came back to taunt you again. It wouldn't have taken much for you to trip him up. You might have thought he had it coming.'

'Huh! You seem to forget that I went down with him. Was I likely to hurl myself to the ground just to make a point?'

'Well, no, but . . . '

Aunt Ruby gave a heavy sigh. 'Do you mind if we change the subject? I'm getting tired of all this and I really would like to get home and put my feet up.'

Nodding agreement, Alyssa inserted the key in the ignition and put the car into gear.

6

With her laptop on the kitchen table, Alyssa was once more struggling to compose her letter to Tom. Somehow the words refused to come. She could think of plenty to say, but it was accusatory in tone, and she knew instinctively that recriminations would be out of place now. If she put his back up he probably wouldn't respond. It was with some relief that she heard footsteps on the wooden steps leading up to the back door, followed seconds later by the strident tones of the doorbell.

'Oh, Constable O'Hare!' she said, standing aside to let him enter. 'Or should I say Benjy?' She grinned, visualising a much smaller version of this man sitting on a child-sized chair in Aunt Ruby's classroom.

'Ben will do, ma'am.' He removed his

cap and tucked it under his arm, standing with his chin held high as if he were on parade.

Oh, dear, so we're going to be formal, are we? Was he always like this, or was it just the uniform? 'Please sit down,' Alyssa said. 'I assume you've come to see my aunt? I heard the shower running a while ago, but I expect she'll be down soon, if she can manage to dress without my help.'

'She is, and she did.' Alyssa jumped. She hadn't heard Ruby coming. Ben leapt to his feet as the old lady seated herself at the table, subsiding as she waved her good hand at him.

'I've come to tell you that the boy's parents won't be pressing charges,' Ben explained.

Ruby's eyebrows shot up. 'I should think not, indeed! After all, it was that pesky child's fault. Nothing to do with me! I should hope he was given a good walloping at home, but no doubt the parents didn't dare to lay a finger on him, in case he sued them for child abuse!'

'Ma'am, the only reason they've backed off on this is because his dad is Chuck Ingram.'

'Is that so!'

Alyssa looked puzzled. 'Who is Chuck Ingram?'

'He was in my grade three class,' Ruby said. 'A dear little boy as I recall, but I'm sorry to hear that he hasn't been able to make a better job of raising his own son.'

Ben cleared his throat. 'The child has made a rather damaging accusation, ma'am, and I've been sent here to look into it. He maintains that when he came back in your direction you turned your back on him so you could use your left hand to lash at him with your cane.'

'Stuff and nonsense! If I turned away it was to avoid another set-to with him.'

'According to Carter — that's his name, Carter Ingram — you deliberately thrust your cane into the spokes of the wheel, causing him to crash.'

Ruby sniffed. 'Well, he would say

that, wouldn't he? And how does he explain how I came to be sprawling on the sidewalk if I wasn't knocked off balance by that young pup? Anyway, you don't need to waste your time interrogating me; there were witnesses. The people in the menswear shop saw it all. They came to my aid within minutes.'

'I've already spoken to them, ma'am. They swear they saw nothing. They were drawn to the scene by your screams for help.'

Don't tell me, Alyssa thought, *Aunt Ruby taught those men when they were children at Beegrove Elementary.* But she said nothing.

'So what happens next?' Ruby wondered. 'What sort of punishment will this Connor receive?'

'Carter, ma'am. His name is Carter. Well, Chuck is making sure that the boy will write to apologise, and on top of that he's lost his television and computer privileges for a week. And because he's been riding on the sidewalk, which is an offence, he has to attend the bike rally next week.'

'Hardly a punishment,' Ruby murmured. 'The police hold this rally each year,' she told Alyssa. 'They test the kiddies on road safety, check their bicycles and helmets, and then send them through an obstacle course, with prizes. It's all great fun, and possibly it prevents accidents in the future.'

'Yes, we have something similar in Mississauga.'

'Then you know all about it, dear.' She turned to Ben O'Hare. 'I've been meaning to let you know that I'll be unable to help you with the rally this year. As you can see, I'm handicapped for the moment, and after my shocking experience yesterday . . . well, I do feel I should take things easy for a while.' She attempted to look pathetic, and failed.

'Quite understandable, ma'am. I'm sure we'll be able to manage somehow.'

Now what was her wily aunt up to? Surely having one arm in a plaster couldn't prevent her from standing on the sidelines, barking out instructions? Alyssa hadn't long to wait before she found out.

'I know that my niece will be glad to help you,' Ruby told Ben, exposing a lot of tooth as she spoke. 'She is a schoolteacher like myself, well used to commanding children. When is this event taking place?'

'Thursday, ma'am, ten a.m. at the Centennial Arena. But we can manage; I'm sure Ms Grant has better things to do with her time.'

'Nonsense! You'll need all the volunteers you can get. You can't have the whole department tied up when they should be out and about solving crimes. Now then, what are you doing this evening, Benjy?'

'Well, er . . . '

That's all right then. We'll expect you for dinner at six. We'll have a nice meal, and then you can put Alyssa in the picture. Explain what she'll be doing at the rally.'

Embarrassed, Alyssa looked down at

her feet. Auntie was so obvious, plotting to bring the two of them together. And what if Ben was in a relationship — married, even? But of course if he were, then Auntie would know about it. There could be no secrets in a place the size of Beegrove. She stole a glance at Ben. He was smirking.

'I can never resist a good home-cooked meal,' he said, standing up to leave.

When he had gone, Alyssa glared at Ruby. 'Did you have to do that, Auntie? You set us up. I was so mortified!'

'Don't be so silly, child. It's not a date; it's a sort of business arrangement. Besides, if we keep him sweet he won't bother looking into my little contretemps any more, which is all to the good.'

Alyssa narrowed her eyes. 'You didn't really cause that bike to crash, did you, Auntie? You didn't do it on purpose?'

'Ask me no questions and I'll tell you no lies.'

'Oh, Auntie, really! I want you to

promise me that you won't do anything like that again. You can't risk injuring another youngster, no matter how naughty he may be.'

'All right! All right! I'm admitting nothing, you understand. This is merely hypothetical. I will never do anything to injure a *child*. Are you satisfied now?'

Ruby, smiling grimly, reminded herself that, apart from little fiends like Carter Ingram, it wasn't really the children who were the problem. As she knew from speaking to little ones at past rallies that it was the parents who encouraged them to ride on the sidewalks, saying that the streets were unsafe for a five-year-old wobbling from side to side. That was a nuisance, but the real culprits were teenagers and even grown men who charged along, weaving in and out of the crowds of Saturday shoppers without a care in the world. Different treatment was needed to put them in their place, and she knew exactly what that was. All she needed was a bottle of red ink.

* * *

Sighing, Alyssa began to attempt her letter to Tom yet again, but she found she couldn't settle to the task. This had nothing to do with the handsome Ben O'Hare, either. She had no need to feel guilty. Why shouldn't she get out and do a bit of community service? Even if she and Tom had been back together, that didn't preclude interacting with other men in the volunteer sector. Besides, it was important that young cyclists should learn the rules of the road, and what better place than a rally run by local police officers? And if she could help to drum the message home to the youngsters, it would be all to the good for the senior citizens of Beegrove.

Having examined her conscience and found it clear, Alyssa thought about Tom, and found her resentment growing. Why should she go running after him when she had done nothing to drive him away? Who did he think he was, treating her family this way? Her parents had gone to a lot of trouble to organise this wedding in Australia where, after all, they were merely visitors. Not that they were complaining about that. In an email meant to be soothing, Anna Grant had issued the usual platitudes, saying that it was better for the young couple to find out now if they weren't suited, rather than to go through an acrimonious divorce later.

'I thought we *were* suited,' Alyssa muttered, remembering this. 'Tom is the one with the doubts, not me. But why couldn't he have been upfront with me, instead of giving me all that male menopausal stuff about needing to find himself?'

It was useless to keep obsessing over this; Alyssa was well aware of that. She closed her laptop with a snap. 'I'm going out for a walk,' she called up the stairs to Aunt Ruby.

'See you later, dear. Have a nice time.'

7

Back in Mississauga, Steven Grant was also feeling restless. He had studied his law books day and night, determined to succeed in his chosen profession, but he'd reached the point where he could read a page without a word of it sinking in.

Perhaps food would set him right. Peering into the fridge, he found nothing more than an empty egg carton, two bottles of mineral water and some wilted broccoli. Cursing, he went to the store cupboard, glaring at the neat rows of canned vegetables and packaged pasta. Nothing of interest there! His sister hadn't had time to go shopping before haring off to see their great-aunt, so he was left in a real mess. Where were the frozen pizzas, the chocolate digestives, the packaged carrot cakes and the coffee beans he needed?

Some action was called for. First, he would go to Wendy's or MacDonald's and fortify himself with a cheeseburger or two. Then he'd go to the supermarket and stock up for the duration. It looked as if Alyssa might not be back for some time, and a guy had to eat.

Standing well back in the lineup for ordering his lunch, Steven glanced around the fast-food restaurant, doing a double take when he noticed a dark-haired girl who had just got up from her table. Wasn't that the female he'd seen with Tom Carson? As he watched she emptied the contents of her tray into the rubbish bin and headed for the exit.

'Hey! Wait a minute! Excuse me! Excuse me!' He thrust his way through the crowded room, crashing into a baby stroller in the process.

'Do you mind, mister?' The young mother glared at him, annoyed.

'Sorry!' he yelled over his shoulder, while continuing to elbow people aside.

Out in the street he peered from side to side, unable to spot the girl. Then a bus pulled up and she darted out of a shop doorway, joining several people who were about to get on. Steven raced in their direction and managed to squeeze in, just as the doors began to close.

'You were cutting it fine, mister!' the driver told him, as the bus began to swing into the line of traffic.

Steven grunted something as he fished in his pocket for a bus token. The girl had taken a seat next to the window, halfway down the bus. He saw with relief that the aisle seat next to her was empty. He could get close to her without it seeming odd.

He stole a covert look at the girl. She had on a scarlet jacket and bootleg jeans over high-heeled black boots. He could not remember what she'd been wearing when he'd caught a glimpse of her with Tom, but the hair was the same both times, curly and shoulder-length. He would have known her anywhere.

He cleared his throat, wondering how to begin. There was no way of knowing how long she'd be on the bus, and if she had plans to switch to another route he'd be in a pickle. He'd been so relieved at having caught up with her, he'd forgotten to ask the driver for a transfer ticket, and he'd given up his last token.

'Excuse me; haven't we met before?' he began.

The girl turned her head, her chin held high. 'No, I don't think so.'

Steven cursed himself for having delivered the classic chat-up line without meaning to. 'But I'm sure I've seen you with my brother-in-law, Tom Carson?'

This time she was interested. 'Your brother-in-law? Oh, but he told me he isn't married. Was that not true?'

Steven's face turned red. This wasn't going well at all. 'He's engaged to Alyssa, my sister,' he mumbled. 'I meant I've been thinking of him as my brother-in-law, that's all. Not that the wedding is likely to take place now, of course.'

'Oh, is it not? That's too bad.'

'Well, you should know!'

'I've no idea what you're talking about, and I don't think I want to know!'

Steven swallowed hard. 'Look here, Ms, er — I don't know what your name is, but I've seen you out and about with Tom, looking pretty close, I must say. Do you mind if I ask you what's going on?'

The girl frowned. 'Yes, I certainly do mind! I don't know who you think you are, interrogating me like this, but I don't have to sit here and listen to it. Now, if you don't mind, this is my stop, and I'm getting off.' She stood and reached for the overhead cable that warned the driver of passengers wishing to alight. Steven stood too, and she brushed past him, swaying with the movement of the bus as it lurched to a halt.

'That went well, fella!' An older man,

seated across the aisle, grinned at Steven.

'I couldn't have put it better myself,' Steven groaned.

'Women, eh? Who knows what goes on in their heads?'

Steven got off at the next stop and hurried back the way they had come, hoping to catch a glimpse of the girl. It was doubtful that he could learn more from her, but if only he could find out where she lived it might lead him to Tom. Not surprisingly, she was nowhere to be seen when he reached the previous stop. It was a semi-commercial area, with lots of small businesses and Victorian houses, which nowadays were divided into apartments or in use as offices for lawyers or dentists. What a wild goose chase this had been! He went into a tobacconist's shop and bought a handful of bus tokens. He was blowed if he was going to hike all the way home.

Later, tucking into a Hungry Man chicken dinner which he'd heated up in the microwave, Steven considered his options. He wanted to help his sister, no question about that. Carson had left her in a bind, having given up her job and her apartment in preparation for her marriage to him. Steven intended to take the guy by the throat and force him to explain himself to Alyssa. He owed her that much.

But when Steven had tried to find Tom earlier, the guy's neighbours had told him that Tom had given up his apartment, which had already been snapped up by a young couple with a baby.

'Gone to Australia, I heard,' one elderly lady had insisted. 'That's where his fiancée comes from, I believe.'

'Are you one of them private detectives?' a woman in curlers had asked. 'What's he done, then? I hope he ain't murdered someone, because we don't want his sort round here, I can tell you that! I used to think he was nice enough; in fact I might have fancied him myself, but that's always the way, ain't it? It's the ones who look normal that's got something to hide.'

Now Steven tried to make sense of everything he'd been told. Was it possible that Tom had indeed gone to Australia? Perhaps he'd sorted himself out and was prepared to go through with the wedding. Now he was following Alyssa to Australia to make up with her.

But there were flaws in that line of thinking. What would lead Tom to suppose that Alyssa had in fact gone to join her parents? All he needed to do was ask her, but apparently he wasn't responding to her emails or answering his voice mail. Perhaps he meant his reappearance to be a surprise? He would show up on the Grants' doorstep with a bunch of flowers in his hand, and Alyssa would fall into his arms, overcome by this romantic gesture.

Steven considered what the neighbour had said, about a private detective. Should they hire one to trace Tom Carson? But Steven, in debt for thousands of dollars' worth of student loans, could not afford that, and he could hardly take on the task himself, like a sort of Canadian version of Hercule Poirot.

Besides, Alyssa might not thank him for meddling, particularly if it all ended in tears. He made up his mind to go down to this Beegrove place and have it out with her. No doubt this unknown Great-aunt Ruby would welcome him, particularly if he was able to do a few jobs around the place, and between the pair of them she and Alyssa would be able to provide a few decent meals.

Whistling, he went into his bedroom to throw a few garments into a kitbag.

8

Alyssa drove to the cycle rally, half distracted. Numerous unconnected thoughts went through her mind, all seemingly going nowhere. A small girl on a bicycle, veering from side to side, took up most of the single lane in front of her. It was too dangerous to pass; the child might get clipped during one of her movements to the left.

She sighed. A long line of vehicles stretched out behind her, just the sort of situation where an impatient driver might overtake several cars at once. It happened suddenly. The child made a turn to the left to enter Bank Street. No signal whatsoever. Not even a glance behind her. Alyssa jammed on the brakes, causing a blare of horns at the rear.

Flipping on her hazard flashers she pulled over to the kerb, where she came to a halt with her heart pounding. Fortunately all those behind her seemed to have come through the incident unscathed. As the line of cars passed by her she was aware of frowns and mouthed insults from their drivers. She grimaced in return. What was the matter with everyone? Hadn't they noticed what she'd had to deal with?

Shaking, she waited until the road was clear in both directions before driving on. The arena was some miles outside the town and was used by people from the surrounding townships as well as the people of Beegrove itself.

'We're very proud of it,' Aunt Ruby had explained. 'It was built to celebrate Canada's Centennial in 1967. I was teaching then, of course, and I was on the fund-raising committee. The arena itself is used for ice hockey and figure skating, but there are outdoor facilities as well. They added tennis courts in the 1980s and a softball pitch. People of all ages use the arena, so it adds a great deal to the life of the town.'

The police had almost completed their preparations by the time Alyssa arrived at the venue. Ben O'Hare came forward to greet her, smartly dressed in uniform like all his colleagues, bare-armed in short-sleeved shirts with the departmental crest on one shoulder.

'Glad you could make it, ma'am!'

'Alyssa, please. And for a while there it was touch and go!' She told him about her frightening experience. 'No signals, no attention paid to what might have been coming behind her, and she wasn't even wearing a helmet.'

'That's why we hold these things, to try to push some sense into these kids. We try to make the day fun for them, but of course our real aim to is to prevent accidents in the future. I'll never forget the time I had to attend an accident scene where a young cyclist was killed outright, knocked off his bike by a transport truck. That's something I never want to see again, and if giving up my off-duty time to come to this rally helps to prevent it, I'm all for it.'

One section of the field had been cordoned off and Alyssa was directed to a section where traffic cones had been arranged as a slalom course. Her job was to watch each child as he or she navigated the course, deducting a point from a starting total of ten each time one of the markers was knocked over. Most of them did surprisingly well, apart from one poor boy who managed to displace the cones every time.

'It's not fair!' he sniveled. 'You've put them too close together, miss!'

Alyssa, who'd had nothing to do with setting them up, felt sorry for the child. 'We'll let you try again, shall we?' she suggested. This time he managed to struggle around the course with only two disasters. He was obviously one of those uncoordinated children who found physical activities difficult. She was tempted to move the cones further apart to give him a better chance, but she reminded herself that the purpose of the event was to make the children safer on the roads.

As she watched one child after another going through the course, making notes on the cards they handed her, she kept a watchful eye out for the little girl who had so nearly caused a traffic pile-up, but there was no sign of her. Attendance at the event wasn't compulsory, although Alyssa felt that it should be. She made a mental note to discuss the issue with Ben later on.

Ben! She was already thinking of him as Ben, rather than as Constable O'Hare. She reminded herself that the man was a professional. She mustn't get into the habit of chatting to him as if he were a friend, although Aunt Ruby would no doubt approve. And what did she know about the man, anyway? He might be married, or engaged. Of course, Ruby Watson would know all about that, and she would hardly have thrown them together if Ben weren't free.

A whistle blast broke into her reverie. Everyone was being shepherded into the ball diamond, where the children were seated on the grass. A burly sergeant spoke to the assembled children, praising them for taking part and for doing well at the various activities set up for them.

'Some of you have been given notes to take home with you. Some of your bikes don't have lights or reflectors, and one or two need their brakes seeing to. And if I catch anyone on the road without a bell or horn that works, the fine is eighty-five dollars.'

There were cries of dismay from the young cyclists. 'I only get a buck a week allowance!' one boy shouted. 'I can't pay a fine like that! It would take me eighty-five weeks to pay that, and there's only fifty-two weeks in a year!'

'Then you'd better make sure you get a horn, boy! Explain to your folks it's cheaper that way.'

'Sometimes it's like talking to the wind,' a voice said in Alyssa's ear. 'That's why we have to issue official notes to send home with the kids.' She swung around to find Ben standing beside her. She laughed ruefully.

'If their mothers ever see them! How many times have I sent notes home with children, only to have them go through the washing machine in the pocket of their jeans?'

'I can imagine. What gets me, though, is how so many parents let their kids ride the roads on faulty machines, or with no helmets. Don't they want their kids to be safe?'

Alyssa nodded in agreement. She was still shaken up by her earlier experience, as no doubt Aunt Ruby was by her own mishap.

Now the special constables were handing out crests and certificates to the children. 'That about wraps it up,' Ben said. 'How about joining me for a bite of lunch? Nothing fancy, just a sandwich somewhere, by way of thanking you for your help with the rally.'

'Um, I don't know. Auntie is expecting me for lunch, I think.'

'I don't think so. She called this morning and invited me to lunch at her place, but when I said I meant to take you out somewhere she told me to go ahead, with her blessing.'

'Oh, really!' Alyssa was embarrassed. How could Aunt Ruby drop her in it like this? 'I'm sorry,' she stammered, 'but I don't know if I should. You see, I'm engaged. Well, sort of.'

'Oh, come on, Alyssa. It's only a sandwich, not a trip to Vegas.'

At least he was calling by her name now, rather than ma'am. 'Won't you get into trouble if you take someone to lunch in the middle of your working day?

'Like I told you, this is my day off. Now, I'm going to eat whether you want to or not. I'm going to the Country Kitchen, so if you're coming, hop into your car and follow me there. No strings, okay?

Fifteen minutes later, seated in the tiny restaurant with its checked gingham curtains and tablecloths, Alyssa realised that it was quite pleasant to be sitting with a handsome young man, in full view of the world. Everyone seemed to know Ben, and they all told him hi in passing, accompanied by a quick glance at his pretty young companion.

There was nothing in it, of course, but she had to admit that it was balm to her bruised heart to be out with Ben O'Hare rather than sitting at home, brooding. Any feelings of guilt she might feel were quickly banished to the back of her mind, for Tom Carson hadn't thought twice about taking the raven-haired beauty out on the town while his fiancée was planning their wedding in all innocence.

9

Steven Grant pulled into Maple Street, slowing down as he hunted for number 45. The maddening thing was that few of the houses had numbers on them, added to which there were several empty lots which might or might not be designated with numbers. He was forced to drive down the street twice, hoping that nobody saw and suspected him of planning a burglary.

Finally he noticed a faded 45 on the mailbox beside the front door of a substantial brick house. He had to ring twice before the door was opened, to reveal an elderly woman with her arm in a plaster cast. She looked him up and down with annoyance.

'Mrs Watson? I'm Steven.'

'Not today, thank you!' In one fluid movement the old lady stepped back, shutting the door in his face.

'Well done, Steven!' he muttered. 'A great start, I must say. What now?' He could of course ring the bell again, or hammer on the door, but ladies of her age were inclined to be wary of strange men on their doorsteps, and he didn't want her calling the cops. And where was Alyssa? She was supposed to be looking after the old girl, wasn't she? Hopefully she'd just gone to the shops and would be back soon. He sat down on the concrete step and looked round mournfully.

Twenty minutes later his sister drove in, parking neatly in the narrow driveway beside the house. 'Steven! What are you doing in Beegrove? And why on earth are you sitting out here on the step? Does Auntie know you're here?'

Steven shrugged. 'She took one look at me and closed the door. Do you think you can convince her we're related?'

Alyssa laughed. 'I suppose you didn't think to let her know you were coming?

Never mind. Once she knows you're on the up-and-up she'll be delighted to welcome you into the fold.'

'I'm sorry I shut the door on you,' Aunt Ruby said, not looking sorry at all, when introductions had been made, 'but I really can't be blamed. I've had it up to here with young men showing up unannounced at my door. In the old days it was the Fuller brush man, or discharged soldiers with suitcases full of dusters and shoelaces. Nowadays it's missionaries trying to convert me to their religion. Me, a faithful member of the Presbyterian Church since the day I was born!'

'That's all right,' Steven assured her. 'I suppose I should have phoned, but I wanted it to be a surprise.'

'And so it is, dear! And have you eaten yet? I was just about to get lunch for myself but I'm sure Alyssa will make you something more substantial. I usually make do with a cheese sandwich and a glass of tomato juice. How was your lunch with Benjy, Alyssa?

What did he have to say for himself? Will you be seeing him again?'

Steven frowned at his sister. 'Benjy? Who the heck is Benjy?'

Alyssa smiled sweetly. 'Oh, just one of Auntie's kindergarten pupils.'

He frowned again. 'You took a child out to lunch? Why?'

'It's a long story. Never mind that now. I'm glad to see you and all that, but why are you here? There's nothing wrong with Mom or Dad, is there? I haven't had time to check my emails today.'

'What kind of welcome is that? And no, there's nothing wrong with the folks, as far as I know.'

'Then what *is* it, Steve? You're driving me crazy!'

Aunt Ruby laughed. 'Now, now, kiddies! Birdies in their little nests agree! Alyssa, why don't you make our lunch, and then we'll all sit down and talk about this sensibly, whatever it is that has brought your brother all the way up here from Mississauga.'

When Alyssa had produced a pile of grilled cheese sandwiches, accompanied by tomato juice and coffee, Steve looked at her with a false expression of woe on his face. 'What, no dessert?'

Rolling her eyes, she went to the fridge and removed a large wedge of home-made apple pie, which she slapped down in front of him.

He rolled his eyes in return. 'You know I like my pie à la mode.'

'Don't push it, Steve. Anyway we're all out of ice cream so you'll have to make do with cheese.'

Aunt Ruby had watched this exchange with growing irritation. 'That will do, you two! Settle down, do. And if you don't hurry up and explain yourself, Steven Grant, I'll shake you till your teeth rattle.'

'All right, then,' Steven said, wiping melted cheese off his chin with his paper napkin. 'It's about that girlfriend of Tom's, or whatever she is. I followed her home the other day but she got spooked and I lost her.'

'Why on earth would you do a thing like that?' Alyssa asked. 'You'd better be careful, or she might report you to the cops for stalking.'

'I happened to spot her quite by accident, and then I guess I just got carried away. I thought if I could find out where she lives it might lead us to Tom, who seems to have disappeared. I've been to his place and he's long gone. The apartment has been let to other people. I spoke to the neighbours and the only one I could get any sense out of was an old girl who said she thinks he's gone to Australia.'

'Aw, how romantic,' Ruby said, as she tried to refill her juice glass, holding the bottle in her left hand. 'Drat! I've spilled it all over the tablecloth!' She blotted it with her napkin, muttering under her breath.

'The neighbour was probably repeating old news,' Alyssa said. 'She hadn't heard that the wedding is off.'

'On the other hand,' Ruby suggested, 'he may have got his head together by now and is regretting his actions. Assuming that you have to stay with your parents as planned, he means to turn up there with a red rose in his hand, begging you to forgive and forget.'

'If he has done that, then he's an idiot,' Alyssa muttered. 'He knows I was staying at home; if he wanted to know where I was he could have turned up there! Steven could have told him I'd gone to Beegrove. Anyway, I really don't see what all the fuss is about. My loving fiancé has dumped me, and I really don't care if he's gone to Australia, or Timbuktu!'

'Well, I do!' Steven said. 'He hasn't behaved well at all, and I for one want an explanation. So do you, Lys. How are you supposed to get closure if you don't know why he changed his mind?'

'We know why, Steve. He met this girl and decided she's the one for him. Case closed!'

'Excuse me,' Ruby interjected, 'but we don't know that for a fact, do we? I do think that Steven is right, dear. You won't truly have peace of mind until you know what is behind all this. Nor will you be ready to move on with your life.'

Alyssa was tired of all this discussion. They needed a change of subject. 'Speaking of which, Auntie, why isn't Ben O'Hare married? He's handsome, personable, with a worthwhile career. I should think he would have been snapped up ages ago.'

Ruby's eyes filled with tears. 'He hasn't told you, then? No, I don't suppose he would have. He was engaged once, to a lovely young woman: another former pupil of mine. Unfortunately she was shot, and he lost her. Such a tragedy.'

'Shot! Why? Was she in the police force, then?' Alyssa was stunned. Sadly, this would not have been unusual in Toronto, where random shootings occurred all too often, but here in Beegrove? It didn't bear thinking about.

'No, dear. She was a nurse. It happened during the deer-hunting season, when she was out at her father's farm. Some hunters were trespassing and came too close to the house. Poor Clare was outside, hanging out the washing for her mother. It came out at the inquest that the men were drunk at the time, shooting at anything that moved. One of them testified that they didn't realise there was a house beyond the trees; not that that was any excuse for what happened.'

'How awful! Was she killed outright?'

'No. She lingered on in Beegrove General for a week or so, until her parents made the decision to take her off life support. Ben was at her bedside when she died.'

There was silence then, apart from Ruby's small sobs, and Alyssa crossed the room to place an arm around her aunt's shaking shoulders.

'I think I'll just go outside and um . . . ' Steven began, but, on receiving no answer, he pushed his chair away from the table and left. The sad little tale had unsettled him, and he was at a loss as to how to offer comfort to the elderly woman.

10

Ruby Watson carefully looked both ways before crossing Main Street. It was bad enough being jostled aside by children on small bicycles, but there was an even greater danger from careless teenagers. In a way she could understand why parents encouraged young children to ride on the sidewalks, but that did not excuse strapping teenagers, who were far rougher and speedier. In a year or two most of them would be eligible to drive cars, and what then? Obviously they'd stay away from pedestrian areas, but the bad habits learned in their younger days would most likely translate into careless driving.

The powers that be were aware of this, and a system of graduated licenses had been introduced so that new drivers were not allowed unlimited freedom until they were more experienced. Even so, many teens drove as if they were on a racetrack, and the police could not be everywhere. She had explained this to Alyssa.

'If these youngsters manage to get hold of liquor it magnifies the problem ten times over. Last year after high school graduation we had a terrible accident just outside Beegrove. A carload of teens, out celebrating, finished up against a tree. Three of them were killed outright and another is maimed for life. I know every one of their parents, of course. Benjy told me that it was caused by a combination of high speed and alcohol. Tragic, and so unnecessary.'

Alyssa winced. The story was all too familiar.

'I don't know what the answer is, dear, I really don't. They all take driver education classes at school, and I'm sure the instructor gives them a good talking-to about safety issues, but nothing seems to sink in.'

Now Ruby was meandering down Main Street, looking at all the changes that had taken place in the past few years. When she had come to Beegrove as a young bride, this street had held a multitude of little shops — a grocery store, a butcher's shop, a milliner's and a toy shop, among others. All gone now, of course, since the mall had been built on the other side of town, and even there the selection was limited because you could order most things through the Sears catalogue if you didn't want to travel to the city.

She stopped in front of what used to be the stationer's but was now Brody's Office Supplies. Taking a deep breath, she went inside.

'How may I help you?' The bored teenager parroted the words with a distinct lack of enthusiasm.

'I'd like a bottle of ink, please. Red.'

'Ink?'

'Yes. You know, the stuff you write with.'

The girl looked puzzled. 'I don't

think we sell that. We do have ballpoint pens in a selection of colours. Can I show you some?'

'No, that won't do at all. It has to be ink.'

'What did you want it for? I don't think anybody writes letters any more. Everyone sends emails or text messages now.'

'Well, I don't. And I don't wish to write a letter. I'm taking up calligraphy.'

'Ca-what?'

'The art of beautiful writing, dear.'

'Oh. Then you could try Simpson's Art Supplies, halfway up the street on the other side.'

'I don't think I . . . '

'My Gran told me it used to be a sort of toilet or something.'

'Yes, yes. I know what you mean now,' Ruby told her.

Plodding back up the street, she told herself that she must indeed be getting old if she'd forgotten that. Years ago there had been public lavatories in that building, and a room with couches where tired shoppers could take a break. The facilities were chiefly intended for the farmers and their wives who came in from the country to shop. No doubt they were grateful for such a place after a long, cold drive in an open buggy. The place had been closed in the nineteen sixties when, presumably, cars made journeys shorter.

The art supply shop was a treasure trove of everything the budding artist might need. It held everything from paint-by-numbers sets to a bewildering variety of acrylics, watercolours and oil paints. Paintings by local artists dominated the walls. Ruby noted that some looked most professional while others, to her untrained eye at least, appeared to be mere daubs.

The woman in charge shook her head regretfully when Ruby repeated her spiel. 'You know, I have no idea whether they even make red ink any more, or green, for that matter. Now I do have some calligraphy sets for beginners here, twenty per cent off! Can I interest you in one of those?'

But Ruby had had enough. 'No, thank you. You're very kind, but I think I'll wait until I get this silly cast off, and see how I feel then. I'm told I have to get physiotherapy, but until the time comes I shan't know how much mobility I'll recover. I'm eighty-three, and nothing is certain at my age. It was silly of me to think about buying craft supplies at this time.'

'I quite understand, and I hope you make a full recovery. If you'd like to come back when you know more, I'll be glad to assist you to find something you'll enjoy. Calligraphy might be too much for you if your fingers are a bit stiff, but we do stock some very nice jigsaw puzzles. Many of our older customers enjoy doing those and if you get too tired you can always leave them for a while and return to them later.'

Ruby thanked her and left, feeling guilty. So red ink seemed to be a lost cause. She'd have to think of something else. Cranberry juice? No, too thin.

Ketchup? No, that would clog up the water pistol. Would tomato juice do the trick? She had some of that at home. She would try it and see.

Her mind turned to Alyssa and Steven, waiting for her at home. She smiled. They were such nice young people. Dear Alyssa had set aside her own troubles and rushed to Beegrove to assist her great-aunt, even though they had never met. Young Steven seemed equally sympathetic, trying to help his sister in her hour of need. Anna Grant had done a good job of raising those two. It was a great pity that so many of the parents in today's generation were failing their offspring by not setting a similar good example.

Ruby stopped for a moment to rest her legs. Surely there was more that she could do? As a retired school-teacher she was well equipped to go on the lecture circuit: why shouldn't she tour the women's institutes and church societies to get them fired up about How We Are Failing The Youth of

Today? No, forget that. Better make it How We Are Failing The Leaders Of Tomorrow. She sighed. Most of the women in those groups were grandmothers. It would be preaching to the converted. It would be better to revert to Plan A.

11

'Do stay for a few more days,' Ruby told Steven. 'You are most welcome. I'm so pleased to be getting to know my nephew's children at last.'

'That's very kind, Auntie, but I must be getting back to Pookie and Rybena. Mrs Flanagan — that's Mom's cleaning lady — has been popping in to feed them for me, but isn't up to giving Pookie the proper walks he needs.'

'I understand, but you must come again.'

'Thank you; I'd like that.'

'And of course if I'm ever in trouble with the law, having a barrister in the family might come in handy!'

Steven grinned. 'Are you planning a life of crime, then?'

'You don't know the half of it!' Alyssa raised her eyes to the ceiling.

'And what are your plans, Lys? Would

you like me to keep searching for Tom?'

She shrugged. 'Please yourself. As far as I'm concerned, Tom Carson can go jump in Lake Ontario.'

'Come on, you don't mean that!'

'Well, how would you feel under the circumstances?'

'Look, I know you're hurt. Who wouldn't be? But do you want to spend the rest of your life wondering why?'

Alyssa had scarcely thought of anything else, and she knew it wasn't healthy. Tom had committed himself to marrying her, to spending the rest of his life in her company, and all of a sudden he had forgotten that and had transferred his affections to somebody new. Was this other girl better looking, more intelligent, wittier or more charming than Alyssa? Had she managed to seduce him in an unguarded moment so that he was now in thrall to her? These ideas didn't do much for Alyssa's self-esteem.

What if Tom had confessed any of this? Would she have begged him to reconsider? And if he had done so, would she have been able to trust him again? Perhaps he wasn't the man she had thought he was, and she'd had a narrow escape.

'I suppose I would like to know why he dumped me,' she said at last, biting her lip.

'Then Steven must track the man down and demand that he speak to you,' Ruby announced. 'Once we get that over and done with you'll feel free to see more of young Benjy.'

'Oh, Auntie!'

'Never mind 'oh auntie'. You could travel far from here and not find another like him. I've known him since he was knee-high to a grasshopper, and I can tell you this: there is no finer a person than Benjamin O'Hare.'

'I'm sure he'd be glad to know what you think of him.'

'Don't be sarcastic with me, young lady!' Auntie snapped, very much the schoolteacher.

Steven stood up. 'Right, then! We're

in agreement, are we, Lys? I'm to go back and look for Tom. The only thing is, where do I start? Do you think that Ben could do something in his official capacity?'

'Like what? We've no reason to think that he's a missing person. The police would only say that he's over eighteen and a competent adult. He's free to go wherever he likes and if he chooses to sever all ties with his friends, that's his privilege. We have no reason to feel that he's in danger, and we don't suspect that he's met with foul play. No, that's a non-starter, Steve.'

'But surely it's worth a try? He might be on their computer or something.'

'I shouldn't think he's ever committed a crime, or had his fingerprints taken.'

'Computers!' Aunt Ruby said. 'What about that internet thing? Can't you go on it and Boogle his name and track him down that way?'

'Google, Auntie. It's called Google. I don't think that will help in this case. I tell you what, though; you've given me an idea. I'll try Facebook. Does Tom have an account, Lys?'

She shrugged. 'Not as far as I know, but I'm only the discarded girlfriend.'

'Never mind. I'll post messages on mine. Somebody out there is bound to know something. Do you have a photo of him, by any chance?'

Alyssa reached for her wallet. She still had a couple of snaps in there; one showed the pair of them in happier days, and the other was Tom's university graduation picture. So many times she'd taken them out, meaning to tear them to shreds, yet something in her sad heart had always insisted she keep them. Wordlessly, she handed the grad photo to her brother.

'Right, then! I'll be off, and as soon as I get home I'll get to work.'

'Not at the expense of your studies, my boy,' Ruby advised.

Steven grinned and saluted. 'Right you are, Auntie! Rest assured, I'll hang on your every word. No beer, no pizza,

just work, work, work!'
'Cheeky!'

* * *

Driving back to Mississauga, Steven considered the wording he might use on Facebook. The photo of Tom would speak for itself. 'Have you seen this man?' might be too dramatic. 'Seeking the whereabouts of Tom Carson' sounded too much like an old British mystery novel. Besides, it was no use sending out the old come-on, beloved of old-fashioned lawyers, to the effect that Tom would 'learn something to his advantage' if he got in touch. What he actually deserved was a kick in the seat of the pants, which Steve would be happy to administer, having seen the sad expression on Alyssa's face when Tom's name was mentioned.

He eventually kept it plain and simple. He uploaded Tom's photo with the words 'Does anybody know where Tom is?' After that it was surprisingly easy. Emails poured into his inbox. Some, of course, were useless; Tom had gone to Australia, got married or had left his place of work. All outdated information. However, the prize was a communication from the man himself, apparently sent from an unknown Yahoo address.

'What's up, doc? Dixie saw your post on Facebook.'

'Where are you, guy, and who the heck is Dixie?' Steven punched in the words and then erased them before he hit the reply button. There was no point in spooking the man right off the bat. If he retreated into the woodwork now he might never emerge again.

'We're all worried about you,' he lied. 'Break-ups are never easy and as you seem to have gone into hiding we hoped you weren't depressed or something. How are you getting on? Can we meet?'

'How about Tuesday? There's a fast food joint on Grenadier Avenue where I like to eat lunch. Don't worry about

Dixie. She has a temp job for an estate agency and she'll be tied up all day.'

'Okay. See you, guy!'

By now Steven had gathered that Dixie was the new love in Tom's life. He was glad to be able to put a name to the face. He couldn't go on thinking of her as 'the beauty' or 'the black-haired girl.'

* * *

'You're looking well,' Tom said when Steven strode into the restaurant. 'You go and grab a table while I order. What do you want?'

'Double cheeseburger with large fries, and a root beer.'

'Sure thing.'

By the time Tom made it to the table, balancing a tray in each hand, Steven had counted out the money for his meal, ready to pay his share. He wasn't going to be beholden to the man who had hurt Alyssa, nor was he about to treat the guy to lunch.

'Okay,' Tom mumbled, through a

mouthful of burger, 'what's this all about?'

'What do you think? It's about Alyssa, of course. It's bad enough that you called off the wedding at the last moment, without lying to her into the bargain!'

Frowning, Tom wiped ketchup off his chin. 'I didn't lie, old buddy. I told her I needed time to get my head together, and that's the honest truth. This thing with Dixie has knocked me for a loop, good and proper.'

'I bet it has! Well, nobody two-times my sister and gets away with it, especially when she's given up everything in the expectation of an imminent wedding!'

Tom stared at Steven, his expression puzzled. 'I'm not two-timing. Surely you can't think that? Who am I supposed to be messing around with?'

Now it was Steven's turn to look surprised. 'Why, this Dixie, of course.'

'Don't be stupid! There's nothing going on between Dixie and me. She's my sister, you idiot.'

'Huh! Don't give me that! According to Alyssa you're an only child.'

'That's what I thought, until recently.'

'What are you getting at?'

'Look, I don't feel like spilling my guts in here, with everybody and his dog listening in. Let's go for a walk and I'll fill you in. But mind you, it's a long story. Have you got time to listen?'

'I've got time,' Steven said grimly.

12

'How would you like to come with me to a concert in the park?' Ben's voice sounded unsure over the phone.

'Er, what sort of music will it be?'

'A mix of pop and light classics, I expect. A bit of Strauss, and bit of Andrew Lloyd Webber; you know the sort of thing. It's the Beegrove brass band and they never tackle anything highbrow. The old bandstand has just been renovated by the Heritage Society and its being relaunched, if you can call it that.'

'Highbrow wouldn't bother me too much; it's teen stuff I can't stand. All screech and no words, as Aunt Ruby would say, and for once I agree with her.'

'So you might come, then?'

'Yes, I will, thank you very much. When is it to be?'

'Sunday afternoon, at three. And wear something warm, because the weather forecast calls for cold winds. Shall I call for you, or do you want to meet me there? I'll bring folding chairs.'

'Oh, I'll meet you there, thanks.'

'Right. Then I'll take you out for tea afterwards. There's a nice little place where the woman makes her own scones and muffins.'

While she found herself looking forward to the outing, Alyssa admitted to a feeling of awkwardness about walking through the streets of Beegrove at Ben's side. As a local boy, now one of 'Beegrove's finest', he was known to everyone. She felt they'd all be looking at her and speculating. She had always disliked the idea of being the subject of gossip, perhaps because schoolteachers were expected to be like Caesar's wife, beyond reproach.

Aunt Ruby, of course, was delighted that Alyssa had received another invitation from Ben. To judge by the gleam in her eye it was evident that she already had the pair wedded and bedded. How lovely if this new-found niece would marry poor Benjy and settle down in Beegrove!

'Perhaps you'd like to come with us,' Alyssa suggested. 'You might enjoy the fresh air and the music.'

'Thank you, dear, but no. I want to catch up on some reading, and if I want music I do have my radio.'

'Are you quite sure?'

'Oh, yes. Two's company, three's a crowd. Besides, I might just take a little nap. I can't think why I feel so sleepy these days. It must be those pain pills the doctor has given me.'

With that settled, Alyssa reviewed her meagre wardrobe, wondering what to wear. Having left Mississauga in such a hurry she hadn't packed much and now she had very little choice. What did people wear for a Sunday afternoon outing in Beegrove? Her one pair of jeans seemed too informal and besides, they really needed a wash. She finally settled on a dark blue T-shirt, to be worn with a floral cotton skirt and high-heeled strappy sandals. At the last moment she exchanged the sandals for a pair of espadrilles; she didn't want to break off a heel marching over rough grass.

'Well, aren't we the Bobbsey twins!' Ben exclaimed when they met in front of the bandstand. He, too, wore a T-shirt in the same shade of blue.

'Did you read those books too?' Alyssa asked, intrigued at this glimpse into his childhood.

'For a while, I guess. That is, until I got into the Hardy Boys books. I couldn't get enough of those.'

'Just like me with Nancy Drew,' she said, naming another series of books published by the same company. 'Is that what attracted you to police work, reading about the boy detectives?'

'Actually I had an uncle in the police force, and he convinced me that it would be a worthwhile career.'

'And how has it worked out? Do you find the work interesting?'

Ben pursed his lips. 'I guess so, although not a lot happens in Beegrove. It's mostly petty thefts or drunk driving. Right now we're trying to convince people to lock their cars when they leave them parked. If they don't, it's too much of a temptation for thieves to reach in and take what they want, including the CD player.'

'I always lock my car, even when I'm just popping in to pay for my gas.'

'Ah, yes, but you're from the big city! Around here things are different. The older people have never been used to locking their houses, either. I'm afraid it's going to take something nasty, such as a home invasion, before they come into the twenty-first century.'

A series of discordant sounds told them that the musicians were tuning up. 'Shall we go and find a seat?' Ben asked, waving a hand towards the rows of folding wooden chairs. Together they found a place on the edge of the grass in the shade of some maple trees.

Soon they were swept away on a waft

of music. Alyssa found it all very peaceful and idyllic, even if 'The Skater's Waltz' wasn't totally appropriate for a late summer afternoon.

'That was lovely!' she remarked, when they had stood for 'O Canada' and the musicians were packing up their instruments. 'Such a pleasant way to spend a summer afternoon.'

'And it's not over yet,' Ben reminded her. 'Time to go and eat!'

'You men!' she teased. 'Always thinking of your stomachs!'

He smiled, and when he took her by the hand it felt entirely natural. She realised with great surprise that she hadn't thought of Tom at all since she had climbed out of bed that morning.

'Are you coming in to say hello to Aunt Ruby?' Alyssa asked, when Ben had seen her home.

'I guess I won't disturb her now. She may be asleep. In any case I should get home and give some thought to a report I'm supposed to write. We must do this again, Alyssa. Go out somewhere together, I mean. I believe that was the last concert of the season. We could go hiking up in the hills, maybe, or out for a drive in the area. There's some pretty scenery over Wychcombe way.'

'I'll look forward to it.'

As she went into the house Alyssa found herself humming one of the tunes they'd heard that afternoon.

'You sound happy, dear. Did you have a good time?' Aunt Ruby was in the kitchen, making herself a cup of tea.

'Yes, thank you, but now there's this tune going round and round in my head, and I can't put a name to it. Isn't it maddening when that happens?'

'It's a sign of advancing age, they say,' Ruby teased. 'And I believe it's Dvořák's 'Humoresque'.'

'Oh, of course! What put me off was hearing it played by a brass band instead of a violin or piano; rather ponderously, I thought.'

'Well, I suppose it's free entertainment. Myself, I like to hark back to the days when we girls went to the old bandstand to hear a rousing selection of John Philip Sousa marches. That was just after the war, of course, when our boys were coming home again. Those who were lucky enough to have made it through.' Ruby wiped a tear from the corner of her eye. 'Don't mind me, dear. I'm just a sentimental old woman, dwelling on the past. Tell me about Benjy; what did he think of it all?'

'It's hard to say. He doesn't show his feelings much.'

'Ah, that comes of being a policeman, I expect. They probably train them in the academy to keep themselves to themselves. Well now, dear, you must make it your task to soften him up a bit, outside of work. I know that young man very well and I can see that he's built a hard shell around himself since his poor young fiancée died. If anyone can crack that, you can.'

'I really don't think that's up to me,'

Alyssa protested. 'I'm not some kind of therapist.'

'Of course not, dear, but he has asked you out several times now and that is a most encouraging sign.'

'I don't think we should read too much into that, Auntie. A bicycle rally, a band concert in the park, a couple of meals out; that's not exactly a wild romance.'

'Ah, but it all adds up, don't you think?'

'I'm not sure that I want it adding up. I like Ben as a friend, and that's all. In fact, I don't want to rush into another relationship. What happened with Tom has taught me that I'm not as good a judge of character as I thought I was. I thought we were soul mates, Auntie, but obviously he didn't feel the same. I don't know if I'll ever be able to trust another man.'

'Child, not every man is as worthless as Tom Carson! That louse didn't deserve you, and I hope that new girlfriend of his throws him over as soon as possible. Then he'll know how it feels to be discarded. Oh, yes. He's a beastly cad.'

Alyssa looked up in surprise. 'You've changed your tune! I thought you were all for Steven tracking him down and making everything right again.'

Ruby shook her head. 'I've had time to think, and I believe I was wrong. What's that silly expression all you young people use? He's a waste of space!'

Alyssa, trying to take this in, was unaware that Ruby had crossed her fingers behind her back.

13

'I wish I could think of some way to return the favour to Ben without giving him the wrong idea,' Alyssa said two days later. 'He's treated me to a few outings now and this is the twenty-first century after all. I should be able to do something in return.'

'I don't see what the problem is,' Ruby told her. 'Invite him here for dinner and make him a special pie, or a chocolate layer cake. The way to a man's heart is through his stomach, as my mother used to say.'

'That's true, but I don't want to reach his heart. As I keep trying to tell Mom, we're just friends!'

'Ah, so you've mentioned him to Anna, have you?'

Alyssa laughed at the knowing expression on Ruby's face. 'Not in the way you mean, Auntie. Mom and I email back and forth and naturally she likes to hear of all my doings. There really isn't a lot to tell, other than the day-to-day happenings in Beegrove.'

'I see. Well, how about buying tickets for the benefit dance, and inviting him to go with you?'

'Benefit dance?'

'Yes. Some people out in the country lost their house to a fire last week, and the community is getting together to help them out.'

'I'm not sure,' Alyssa began. She wasn't ready to snuggle into Ben's arms as they slow-danced to an old-time waltz.

'It's line dancing, I believe. Go for it, girl! It might be fun.'

'Well, why not, if it's for charity. It may be good for a few laughs.'

* * *

The outing was a rousing success. During the breaks when everyone clustered around the bar for beer or iced tea Alyssa found herself the centre of attention, chiefly because of her connection to Aunt Ruby. Several of those present were older ladies, members of a regular line-dancing group, and more than one of 'the girls', as they called themselves, wanted to know why Ruby wasn't there.

'Just as well, really,' one of them said. 'I suppose the cast on her arm might have put her off balance and landed her on the floor with a broken hip. Can't be too careful at her age. Still, she could have sat at the back and watched the fun.'

'I guess she didn't want to be a fifth wheel,' another said, with a sly glance at Ben.

'Ben and I are just . . . '

'Going outside for a breath of air,' Ben cut in, taking her by the arm. 'Come along, Alyssa. Now's our chance while the fiddlers are taking a break.'

'What's the matter; did I say something wrong?' she wondered, when they were standing outside under a starry sky.

'No, no. I just wanted to put a crimp in that conversation you were getting into with the old girls back there. I know Vera Brinkley and Susie McGregor. They're the worst gossips in town.'

'So? There wouldn't have been anything to gossip about if you'd let me finish.'

'That depends on what you were planning to say.'

'Why, that we're just friends, of course.'

'Is that all? We've known each other for a few weeks now, and I swear you're beginning to grow on me, Alyssa Grant.'

'Honestly, Ben, I do like you,' she stammered.

'But you don't love me, is that it? Then let's see how you like this!'

When he swept her into his arms and his lips found hers, she stiffened for a moment, wanting to protest, but then she gave herself up to the moment, forgetting all her qualms. As lovers have done since time began, they remained lost in a world of their own that seemed totally remote from the world around them.

The music started up inside in a thunderclap of sound, and they drew apart, as if waking up from a dream. 'We'd better go back inside before the old biddies start wondering what we're up to,' Ben said shakily.

Alyssa did not reply. She simply followed him back into the hall, asking herself what had just happened, as if she didn't know! And how had she allowed it to happen? And what did it all mean?

* * *

Aunt Ruby had waited up, eager to hear all about the evening.

'I met a Mrs Brinkley and a Mrs McGregor. They told me to say they were asking for you.'

'Oh, they were there, were they?'

'And they wondered why you hadn't come with us.'

'Me!' Ruby laughed. 'A fine sight I'd be with this thing on my arm! I can't wait to get it off. My wrist is so itchy I can hardly stand it. I've tried scratching it with a knitting needle, but it doesn't seem to help. Now then: how is young Benjy? I thought you might bring him for coffee. All that stomping about must have been thirsty work.'

'He couldn't stay. He's on early shift tomorrow. Now, if you'll excuse me, Auntie, I need a shower.'

'So that's how it is,' Ruby thought. 'She can't look me in the eye, and I know what that means! She's falling for him, and I only hope he feels the same about her. I know I should hope to see her back with her fiancé, but it would be wonderful to see her married to Benjamin O'Hare, and living here in Beegrove. I wonder what I can do to help the romance along?'

Upstairs, with the cool water cascading over her shoulders, Alyssa tried to make sense of what had happened at the dance. Ben O'Hare was a lovely man, but she knew she had to be careful. While it was good to have someone pleasant to go out with, the relationship must not go any further. She realised that, without meaning to, she had the power to hurt him. If he let down his guard and allowed himself to love again, and she rebuffed him, he would be devastated. The only answer was to cool it. The next time he invited her out she would make some excuse, and eventually he would get the message.

* * *

A week later all her resolve came crashing down. Aunt Ruby had the radio on, tuned in to their local radio station. Alyssa was shelling peas into a bowl on her lap, and Auntie was leaning back in her rocking chair, humming tunelessly in time to the music.

'Endless Wire' came to an abrupt halt

as the voice of the deejay cut in. 'We interrupt this programme to bring you up to date on the hostage situation out on Mill Road. Our reporter, Rob Bryant, is there at the scene. What's the latest, Rob?'

'Well, Pete, the alleged hostage-taker is still inside the house, along with his common-law wife and their two small children. Members of our local police department are at the scene, and a SWAT team are on their way from the city.'

'Thank you, Rob. We'll fill you in later, folks, as soon as we have more to report. Meanwhile, we return to our Gordon Lightfoot special.'

Music filled the air again. 'Can you reach over and switch on the television?' Ruby asked. 'The local news should be on in a minute and we might learn more. And what in the world is a swat team? Sounds like a bunch of men waving fly swatters!'

'I'm afraid it's rather more serious than that,' Alyssa told her as she switched on the set. 'It's short for Special Weapons And Tactics.'

'How clever of you, dear! I thought it must be something like that.'

'Actually, I know what it means because Ben told me.'

Ruby's face fell. 'Oh, no! Benjy! That Rob person said that our local lads are on the scene, so Benjy must be in the thick of it all!'

Sure enough, the story was on the midday news, with cameras focused on an old brick house, the sort of building that had once sheltered a large family, but had since been divided into flats. Out in the street police cruisers stood at the ready, yet there was no sign of their occupants. Presumably the officers were surrounding the house, or were even now inside.

A disembodied voice, belonging to a negotiator with a megaphone, wafted back to the waiting crew. 'Richie Clarke, we have you surrounded. There is no escape. Can you hear me? I urge you to let the woman and children go.

Let them exit by the front door, one at a time, and we promise you they will be safe.'

There was silence, and Ruby and Alyssa held hands while they kept their eyes on the house door. 'I can't bear this!' Ruby whispered. 'I can't watch, in case something goes wrong!'

'Wait a minute, the door is opening!' Alyssa leaned forward in her seat as the door opened a crack and a small boy sidled around the space. Immediately two cameramen rushed forward, while willing hands pulled the toddler to safety.

A sudden crack, followed by shouts from the crowd, shocked the watching women. 'Officer down! Officer down!' they heard. In the confused babble that followed Alyssa tried to make out the name of the injured man, but it was Ruby, more used to the names of Beegrove people, who heard it.

'Oh, Alyssa, dear; it's Benjy! That rotten hostage-taker has shot our poor Benjy! I do hope he's not dead! I couldn't bear it if that poor boy has been killed!'

Alyssa jumped up, reaching for her car keys. 'I'm going over there, Auntie. I have to see for myself.'

'You can't do that, dear. The police don't need onlookers getting in the way. They'll only move you on. And there's a killer on the loose. You could get yourself hurt.'

'I don't care, Auntie. If Ben is injured I have to be with him!' Holding back the tears, she fled from the house. She realised now that she had deep feelings for Ben O'Hare, and if anything had happened to him she needed to be at his side.

Afterwards she could barely remember getting into her car and lurching off down the street. Fortunately there were few vehicles on the road then, because in sleepy old Beegrove everything ground to a halt at lunchtime. People were either indoors or in one of the local restaurants, building up their strength for the afternoon's work that lay ahead.

She parked halfway up Mill Street, propelled herself from the car and began to run towards the brick house. Two uniformed paramedics were just loading a stretcher into an ambulance. Ominously, the patient's face was covered with a blanket. Alyssa covered her face with her hands and began to shake.

14

'This all started back in the spring,' Tom began when he and Steven were seated on an iron bench beneath an oak tree. 'Of course I was still teaching at the college then, although exams were over and I'd already given in my notice because of our plans — Alyssa's and mine, that is. One morning I was busy marking papers and doing the usual end-of-term stuff, but I couldn't seem to settle down. I thought I might go home and do the marking in comfort. I was about to leave when I was paged and asked to go to the administrator's office.'

'Uh huh,' Steven muttered, leaning forward and resting his arms on his knees.

'The secretary told me there was a young lady waiting in the reception area, wanting to see me. My first thought was that Alyssa had come, but no; it was Dixie. Of course I had no idea who she was at the time. She didn't look familiar at all, and she wasn't one of my students. 'Can I help you?' I asked her, hoping to deal with whatever it was she wanted, and get off home.

''I hope you can,' she stammered, 'because I think you're my brother. I'm Dixie Paulsen, and I've been searching for you for such a long time.'

'Of course I told her she'd made a mistake; I'm an only child. I wished her well in her search and tried to leave, but she held onto my arm and insisted I should hear her out.'

'Poor girl. Looking for her birth parents, I guess, like so many others these days.'

'If only it were that simple. No, she knows who her birth parents are; she grew up with them. I'm the one who should have been looking.'

'What?'

'Well to cut a long story short, I'm

not who I thought I was. Not Tom Carson at all, but a totally different chap by the name of Paulsen.'

Steven's jaw dropped. 'It must be some sort of scam. She knows you have a good job and she wants to get money out of you, that's what it'll be. I don't know why you didn't go straight to the police, Tom.'

'So far she hasn't asked me for a thing, and that being the case I don't know why she'd come all the way from Saskatchewan just to tell me a fairy story unless she was sincere.'

Steven rolled his eyes. 'So who is this Paulsen fellow?'

'I told you: I am, according to her. Her mother died of cancer a couple of years ago, and when Dixie was sitting at her bedside at the hospital the woman told her that she, Dixie, had a brother in Toronto and she should look him up.'

'Ah, I see.'

'I know what you're thinking, Steve. This woman had a baby when she was an unmarried teenager and had to give it up for adoption. In other words, me!'

'Well, it's a common enough story isn't it? And what does it really matter, anyway? Aside from the anguish your birth mom must have suffered, I mean, when she had to give you up. Your adoptive parents were the ones who really counted.'

'But according to Dixie, her mother changed her tune and said that she hadn't given birth to me at all. After that things got confused and nothing seemed to make sense any more. The poor woman was on high dosages of morphine and was delirious half the time.'

Steven stared off into the distance, thinking hard. A young woman strolled past with a baby in a buggy, and two little boys raced by, shrieking. 'So the mother dies,' he said at last, 'and this Dixie is all alone in the world. You didn't say where the father is.'

'Did a bunk years ago. Unstable, apparently.'

'Uh huh. So Dixie decided to look

you up. But how? She's searching for Tom Paulsen, a man who doesn't exist. At least, there must be tons of guys with that name, but the world knows you as Tom Carson.'

Tom studied his fingernails. Finally he gave a great sigh and glanced up with such misery in his eyes that Steven had to look away.

'That's the thing, you see. When Dixie was going through her mother's papers she found a note headed 'Tom's parents'. It named my people, Robert Carson and Maura McGregor, with their address in Nova Scotia. As you know, Mom and Dad died in that car accident on the Cabot Trail, so by the time Dixie started her search their house had been sold and I'd come to Toronto. She had to hire a private detective to get her the rest of the way, and here we are.'

Steven stood up, stretching. 'Well, if you don't mind me saying so, none of this excuses what you've done to Alyssa! I can see that it's been a shock for you to find out you were adopted, but a lot of people go through that without going off the deep end. Why didn't you just tell Alyssa about all this? I know she'd have understood if you'd said you needed time to get your head together, but no! You had to make her suffer!' He groaned suddenly. 'Oh, no! I'm as bad, telling her I'd seen you with another woman! Listen, I'll email her and let her know what you've told me. That'll put her out of her misery to some extent. Then I strongly advise you to get in touch. You owe her that much. Even if the wedding is still off at least she'll know that none of this was her fault.'

'You think I should pull myself together, is that it? Dry your tears, be a big boy and tomorrow is another day? It's not as easy as that. I just don't know who I am anymore. As part of our social studies lessons back in elementary school, the teacher had us make up a little family tree. A little chart naming our parents and grandparents, and anything further back we could find out about. I remember sitting with my nan while she told me about all the wonderful Carsons and McGregors — honest, hardworking folks, descended from fishermen and farmers. People to be proud of, she said. Not a bad 'un in the lot. Those were her exact words, Steven. I can hear her yet, telling me the old tales while she got on with her knitting.'

'And she didn't say anything about you being adopted?'

'Obviously not. Which now makes me wonder where I fit in. Why did Dixie's mother have the address of a couple living several thousand miles away? My parents never went to Saskatchewan; at least, not in my lifetime.'

'Why don't we walk on?' Steven suggested. They strolled on, past the paddling pool, past the gazebo where two old men sat smoking pipes and reminiscing, over the ornamental bridge and on towards the tennis courts. His mind was awhirl with possibilities. At last he came to a halt, clapping Tom on the shoulder. 'I guess your birth mom could have been someone the Paulsens knew, say Dixie's aunt, or a cousin. There was a private adoption by the Carsons, so everybody kept in touch.'

'Don't be a fool,' Tom snapped. 'Years ago birth mothers weren't told where their babies went, and as for private adoptions, I doubt they were even legal. Never mind all that! What I'm worried about is the thought that my Dad — that wonderful, gentle man I adored — was somebody I didn't really know at all! He had an affair with this Paulsen woman, and I'm the result. My poor dear mother agreed to take me on and that's how I ended up in Nova Scotia. I don't know what other explanation there could be.'

Steven whistled — a long, low sound that startled a group of ducks swimming on the pond nearby. 'Neither do I. It sounds pretty far-fetched to me.'

'Maybe it does, but what if I'm right, and I take after Dad? My mother

— Maura, that is — was the sweetest person alive. What if the genes come to the fore in me? What if I married Alyssa and ended up letting her down? I just can't risk it.'

'I think you should let her be the judge of that. Now then, are you going to contact her, or do I have to take you by the scruff of the neck and march you down to Beegrove?'

15

Alyssa was staring in horrified fascination at the scene unfolding in front of her when a familiar voice sounded in her ear. 'What the heck are you doing here, woman? This is no place for you.'

An unpleasant fuzziness manifested itself in the top of her head before she slumped to the ground.

* * *

'This one's okay. Looks like she's coming round. Forget about the oxygen.' This was a different voice. Reluctantly, she opened her eyes and tried to smile at the burly paramedic bending over her.

'You're still with us, then, ma'am. You passed out for a moment, but nothing to worry about. We'll take you to emergency by and by, just as soon as we get things sorted out here.'

'No hospital!'

'Well, we'll see how you go on before we make that decision. Meanwhile, we'll find a place for you to sit down, okay? Up you come!'

'Ben?'

'No, I'm Phil.'

'I meant . . . '

'Save it till later, lady, can you? I'm needed back there.'

Someone had produced a kitchen chair for Alyssa to sit on, and she hunched over, rocking slightly, wrapped in a red blanket. Uniformed men were leading a sobbing woman from the house now, and the small hostages ran to her, wailing: a little boy and an even smaller girl. They clung to each other as the television cameras rolled.

Alyssa crouched deeper into the enveloping blanket as a reporter from the *Chronicle* came closer. The last thing she wanted was to appear on the front page of the next issue, described in a caption as 'woman being treated at the scene'.

'So this is where you've got to!' Ben said, sounding annoyed. 'Sorry I couldn't wait around when you hit the dust, but I'm on duty here and I could see you were in safe hands. Now then, do you want to tell me what your game is? This is no place for sightseers!'

'I thought you were dead!' she howled.

'Dead! What gave you that idea?'

'We had the television on and they said an officer had been shot. Auntie said they gave his name as O'Hare. Oh, Ben, I couldn't bear it, so I had to come. And then I saw somebody being carried out on a stretcher with the face covered up . . . '

'Wait a minute,' he interrupted. 'The body you saw was the hostage-taker. Minutes after he tried to shoot his way out, he turned the gun on himself. You'd have been on the road by then, so you wouldn't have known about that.'

'But where are you hurt? You seem all right to me, but they said you were shot.'

Ben frowned. 'Wait a minute. I think I know what's happened. The injured officer is Ray Dellaire. I've noticed that Mrs Watson is becoming hard of hearing; she must have got it wrong. O'Hare, Dellaire; do you see? And Ray's going to be okay. Just a flesh wound, I believe. So you see, you've come rushing over here all for nothing.'

'Now I feel stupid.'

'Oh well, it happens to us all at times. Hang on a minute while I square it with the chief and then I'll run you home.'

* * *

'I shouldn't really be telling you this,' Ben told Alyssa when she was tucked up in the cruiser en route to Aunt Ruby's house, 'but it'll be all over Beegrove by now, the media having been on the spot. So I guess it won't do any harm, as long as you don't go spreading it about that you got the word from me.'

'Of course I won't do any such

thing,' Alyssa agreed, having recovered sufficiently to be curious.

'It's the same old story. There's an abusive husband, and a wife who can't bring herself to turn him in, so she keeps returning for more. We've been called to a 'domestic' at that place a number of times, but the woman finally had enough and took herself and the kids to a women's shelter. We'll know about it in time, but it seems that for whatever reason, she went back to the guy and the situation just boiled over. When the negotiator was trying to defuse the situation the husband kept shouting that he wasn't going to let the wife take his kids away from him. He'd kill the lot of them first and take a few of us with him.'

'How sad.'

'That's love and marriage for you. Here we are, Alyssa. Can you make it to the door by yourself? You'll have to excuse me if I don't come in. I'm still on duty, eh?'

Still feeling a bit wobbly, Alyssa stood

at the roadside, watching him drive away. Was he mad at her? Embarrassed? He hadn't even given her his customary 'See ya!'.

The kitchen door opened. 'Alyssa! Alyssa!'

'Coming, Auntie.' Wearily, she plodded to the door, desperate to get inside and up to bed.

'Where were you? What happened? Wasn't that Benjy? Is he all right? Talk to me, girl! I've been worried out of my mind, and those reporters on the television are making no sense whatsoever, just milking the drama for all it's worth!'

Alyssa allowed Aunt Ruby to guide her to the sagging couch in the kitchen. Then, covered with a bright green afghan and holding a mug of hot, sweet tea in her shaking hands, she repeated what Ben had told her.

'Oh, I feel such a fool!' Ruby twittered. 'I could have sworn they said O'Hare, but you say it's a fellow called Dellaire, and he's going to be fine?

Thank goodness for that! Mind you, I did say you shouldn't go on over there, didn't I? But you had to go right ahead, didn't you, you silly girl.'

Lost in thought, Alyssa continued to sip her tea.

'Perhaps I shouldn't state the obvious,' Ruby said at last, 'but it seems to me that you've developed feelings for young Benjy. Am I right?'

'I suppose I've become fond of him, as a friend.'

Ruby looked at her over the top of her bifocals. 'And that's all it is?'

'Oh, I don't know, Auntie! I'm so confused. After being let down by Tom, practically on the eve of our wedding, I felt I'd better steer clear of any romantic involvement for a while. Now this.'

Ruby nodded happily. 'As you say, there's no need to rush into anything. Just go along quietly as you and Ben have been doing, keeping your relationship low key, and we'll see where it might lead.'

'Probably nowhere,' Alyssa said, looking gloomy. 'He rushed off without even saying 'see you later'. After this morning's little debacle he probably doesn't want to see me again.'

'Nonsense, dear. He's just been involved in a huge drama at work, and he has to get back there now and help to pick up the pieces. Naturally he can't be thinking of romance at a time like this. Just give him a few days and he'll be on the doorstep, wanting you to go somewhere interesting with him. This is the season for fall fairs and he's always been keen on cattle-judging and those events where collie dogs round up sheep and herd them into pens. Fear not, my girl, love will always come a-calling.'

Alyssa smiled weakly at this, but her bruised heart would not let her share the old lady's optimism. And her fears proved to be right. The days passed, and there was no word from Ben. Ruby had something to say about that, too.

'This is the twenty-first century, my

girl. Why sit here moping like a Victorian maiden, wondering why he doesn't call? There's nothing to stop you from contacting him. Invite him here for supper. You can make a big pan of lasagna and serve it up with salad and hot rolls. He loves lasagna, and I know that for a fact.'

'It's kind of you to suggest it, Auntie, but I think I'd just like to wait and see.'

'Very well, child. It's your life, and your choice. Just don't come crying to me if the man slips through your fingers because you were too timid to take action!'

Alyssa knew that Ruby was only trying to help, but there was something she had to work out for herself. She had rushed to Ben's side because she believed he was dead, or injured, and she knew that the world would be a desolate place indeed if he was stolen from her life. Her grief had been genuine. But when she had been sitting beside the ambulance, draped in a red blanket, her thoughts had flown to

Tom. She had known then that if he, too, were in a potentially deadly situation she would be so devastated that she wouldn't want to go on.

Tom was lost to her now for unfathomable reasons, and some day she would come to terms with that. Meanwhile, it would be wrong to put Ben O'Hare in the role of second-best. He deserved better than that.

16

'I'm just going out to Wal-Mart,' Aunt Ruby said. 'Is there anything I can pick up for you, dear?'

Alyssa thought for a moment. 'I guess there's nothing I need, thank you, but would you like me to drive you there?'

'No, thank you, dear. I'll get the Sunbeam bus.' This was a mini-bus, run by a local charity, which provided twice-weekly transportation for seniors who wanted to go to the shopping mall outside the town. While some liked to go shopping, many of the older people used the trip as a social occasion, meeting their friends for coffee and doughnuts at the open cafeteria. Others joined in the weekly 'Walk for Health,' marching around the indoor walkway, chatting and laughing as they went.

'But won't you have a lot to carry up from Main Street?'

'No, no; I just need a few bits and pieces. They'll fit nicely into my tote bag.'

'All right, then, if you're sure.'

Alyssa watched from the front window as Ruby set off down the street, waving her stick in a jaunty manner. Satisfied that the old lady was in fine fettle, she went back to her laptop, meaning to write to her mother.

For her part, Ruby was thankful she'd persuaded the girl to stay at home. She really didn't want to be seen buying that water pistol, and still less did she wish to concoct a reason for why she needed it.

When she entered the superstore she made her way to the toy department, first turning down a request from two church ladies to buy raffle tickets. She paused at a special display of arthritis remedies before moving on. The special price tempted her, but her medicine cabinet was already full of the stuff and there was no point in spending good money on more.

The water pistols they had on offer were small, and she was annoyed to find that the swollen knuckle on the index finger of her left hand prevented her from activating the trigger. Some large guns on an upper shelf caught her eye. Could she manage one of those?

As she reached up she noticed a boy eyeing some miniature vehicles. Her long experience of teaching allowed her to judge that he was perhaps eight years old. There was something furtive about the child and here again her teacher's instincts told her that he was up to something he shouldn't have been. Sure enough, a chubby hand reached out and a tiny red truck was transferred to his pocket and he moved away down the aisle, his expression bland.

Ruby acted without thinking. 'Stop that boy!' she roared, just as an associate rounded the corner of the display. Spooked, the boy charged past the woman in the blue waistcoat, causing her to crash into a shelf of plastic baseball bats.

'Oh, darn!' Ruby moaned. 'Can't you do something? Look, he's getting away!'

Looking back over his shoulder, the child had the temerity to stick out his tongue at the two women, and this was his undoing. A male shopper skillfully manoeuvred his shopping cart into the path of the fugitive, who lost his balance and fell to the floor. At this point the store manager came hurrying up, and the boy was led away, with Ruby following.

The man with the cart gave Ruby the thumbs-up sign as she bustled past. 'Grey power!' he exclaimed. 'One up for the oldies!' Ruby grinned back at him. He was her kind of good citizen!

In the office the child denied everything. 'He's lying, of course,' Ruby said. 'I saw him putting a toy into his pocket, and by the look of that bulge under the bib of his overalls there's something in there besides his chest.'

'You can't keep me here!' the boy howled. 'I haven't done nothing!'

'You haven't done *anything*,' Ruby

corrected, ever the schoolteacher.

'That's what I said, dumbo! I want my lawyer!'

'You've been watching too much television, son,' the manager said, clamping a large hand on the boy's shoulder. 'Let's have a look inside your pockets, shall we?'

The child shook him off. 'Don't touch me, you pervert! My dad will sue you!'

Sighing, the manager stood back. 'I tell you what, kid; you give me the things you took and we'll let you go, if you promise to stay out of my store in future. All right?'

Sullenly, the boy produced the little car, which he slapped into the manager's hand.

'And the rest!' Ruby said. 'Let's see what you have inside those overalls.'

The child slowly removed a box containing a kit for making a model car, which he handed to Ruby. Then he darted away and was lost to sight among the Saturday shopping crowds.

'That was a great success, I must say!' Ruby snapped.

The manager looked at her wearily. 'This happens all the time, ma'am, and it's hardly worth the effort of prosecuting. The courts have enough to do, dealing with real offenders. Kids like this usually get off with a caution, or maybe get probation. When they're under sixteen the newspapers can't print their names, so young thieves are protected at every turn, and you heard what the little devil said. If you happen to grab them when you've caught them in the act, they can make a big song and dance, tell a lot of lies, and have you in the dock for inappropriate touching.'

'It's isn't right!'

'I'll tell you what isn't right, ma'am. It's all these adult shoplifters we get here. Just last week one dame tried to walk out of here carrying a TV set she hadn't paid for. Can you imagine?'

'I can indeed,' Ruby replied. 'Little thieves grow up to be big thieves, and something needs to be done about it.'

Still muttering about the shortcomings of modern society, she picked up a copy of *Hello!* magazine and took it to the checkout.

'Did you find everything you wanted today?' the woman parroted, as she accepted Ruby's ten-dollar bill and made change.

'Yes, thank you.'

'Thank you. Have a nice day.'

It was only when she was on the bus, listening with scant attention to the chattering woman sitting beside her, that Ruby realized she had forgotten the water pistol. That was the trouble with getting older, she admitted to herself; you set out to do something, only to find when you got where you were going that you had no idea of what that was. The Golden Years, they called them. What a crock!

* * *

Alyssa looked up when Ruby entered the kitchen. 'Hello, Auntie! Did you have a nice time?'

'No, not really. I stopped a boy shoplifting but he got away with it.'

'That's good.'

Ruby stared. 'And then his arm broke off at the wrist and he put it in his pocket.'

'Uh huh.'

'Alyssa Grant, what is the matter with you? Didn't you hear what I just said?'

'I'm sorry, Auntie. What was that again?'

'It's not important. Has something happened while I was gone? There's nothing the matter with your parents, is here? You told me you planned to email them today.'

'They're okay as far as I know. Actually I haven't got that far yet. When I booted up I found an email from Steven, and we've been chatting back and forth ever since.'

'And what does he have to say for himself? I should have thought he'd have his head down, getting on with his studies, not wasting the whole morning talking to you.'

'He's found Tom, Auntie, and it's really most peculiar.'

17

'That sounds serious, and serious business calls for sensible preparation,' Ruby said. 'You make us a nice strong cup of tea, and I'll see if I can find that box of shortbread I've put by for a special occasion. Now what did I do with it? Ah, yes; it's in the back of the linen cupboard. Do you mind running upstairs to fetch it? Your legs are younger than mine.'

'That's a funny place to keep cookies, Auntie. Did you want to keep them handy in case you feel hungry in the night?'

'It's to keep them out of temptation's way when I'm down here. They are so good, made with real butter, but they tend to go straight to the hips, if you know what I mean.'

Within minutes the pair had the pretty tartan tin open and were making inroads into the contents. 'I fell in love with the picture on this tin,' Ruby said. 'Bonnie Prince Charlie, such a romantic figure, don't you think? And speaking of romance, what's all this about your Tom?'

'As I mentioned, Steve managed to track him down,' Alyssa said. 'Like me, Tom gave up his job and let his apartment go, in the expectation of going to Australia to be married.' Unexpectedly, her voice faltered, and she dabbed at her eyes with a tissue.

'Take another cookie!' Auntie advised, thrusting the tin under Alyssa's nose. 'There's nothing like comfort food when the heart is sore.'

'And that's exactly why the weight-loss industry is thriving in this country,' Alyssa mumbled, through a mouthful of crumbs. 'Of course after we split up I had no way of knowing where he intended to live, but I assumed he'd dig in with friends until he found somewhere else. As it turns out, he was staying with Dixie Paulsen.'

'Dixie who?'

'Paulsen. Apparently that's the name of the girl that Steve had seen him around town with. The one I've been calling the Beauty, for want of a better title.'

'Well, I'm shocked! All I can say is, you've had a narrow escape, dear. And how long has he been associating with this young woman? Does anybody know? Why, if it hadn't been for your brother seeing the pair of them you might have gone through with this marriage, only to regret it later! If he'd carry on with another woman when you were merely engaged, and supposedly deeply in love, heaven knows what he might have done when you were married!' Ruby placed a hand on Alyssa's clenched fingers in a gesture of solidarity.

'At least he wasn't guilty of that,' Alyssa said, reaching for another triangle of shortbread. 'According to Steven, this Dixie is Tom's sister. Well half-sister, anyway.'

'Didn't you tell me he was an only child?' Ruby asked, frowning.

'That's right, and if what Steve says is true, that's what Tom believed. This came completely out of the blue and now he doesn't know what to think.'

'And this Dixie person. Who is she? Where has she come from?'

'Somewhere in Saskatchewan, I think. And she knew nothing of Tom's existence until her mother died, making some sort of deathbed confession.'

'Adopted, I suppose,' Aunt Ruby said, nodding sagely. 'Hoping to find her birth mother now. I understand there's a lot of that happening these days. Does she have documentary proof of anything? That's what I'd want to know.'

'Search me! The whole thing seems rather confused and I'm not sure that Steve fully understands it, either. The point being that Tom hardly knows how to handle it, much less confide in anybody else.'

'And that's why he kept telling you

he needed to find out who he is? Perhaps it was the shock of learning about secrets in his family background, things which may have affected his perception of the way things are. Could he have been adopted, too? That really would have put the cat among the pigeons if he'd reached the age of twenty-nine without the slightest suspicion!'

Alyssa said nothing. A tentative smile reached Ruby's lips, quickly suppressed. For a while there was no sound in the kitchen apart from the ticking of the clock.

'So what do you mean to do next, dear?'

'I don't know what you mean, Auntie. It's up to Tom, isn't it? He's never responded to my emails, never attempted to get in touch. If it hadn't been for Steve, I shouldn't know anything now. As far as I can see, Tom hasn't given a thought to what I may have been going through. Well, the ball is in his court now. If he wants to speak to me, he knows where I am.'

'Isn't that a little harsh, dear? Perhaps a sympathetic ear is just what's needed now. Couldn't you find it in your heart to extend a helping hand to the poor boy?'

'Steve says that he tried to convince Tom to get in touch with me, but has he bothered? No! Not a word. I'm not stupid, Auntie Ruby. I can get the message as well as the next person. You don't know Tom Carson like I do. Once his mind is made up it's like the Rock of Gibraltar, solid and unmovable. I know when to quit, that's all.'

'I expect you know best, dear,' Ruby said, taking the lid off the teapot and peering inside. 'It looks as if the well has run dry. Do we want another pot, I wonder, or is it too close to lunchtime?'

'I think I'd like to take a walk, if you don't mind.'

'Of course, dear. I'm sure you have a lot of thinking to do. I'll probably take a nap while you're gone, so don't worry if you don't see me when you come in.'

* * *

But sleep eluded Ruby when she lay down, even though she placed a sleep mask over her eyes to ward off the sunlight that filled the room. After a while she threw off the duvet and struggled to a sitting position with her legs over the side of the bed.

She had become fond of Alyssa during the few weeks they had been together. It was so good of the girl to have hurried up to Beegrove to help an aged relative she'd never met before. Ruby wished she might do something in return, for the girl was plainly unhappy.

A little voice in her head told her that she mustn't interfere in the private lives of other people. She ignored it. Why shouldn't she give love a helping hand? Here were the two young people she loved most in all the world, pining away for want of a little encouragement. Benjamin O'Hare was kindly, pleasant, hard-working and bereaved. The same could be said of Alyssa, in a way. If they could be brought together, how wonderful that would be! But how to achieve that happy outcome?

That Tom Carson was the fly in the ointment, of course. Before she did anything else, Ruby thought, she must take steps to find out if that relationship was really as dead as it seemed. And in order to get to the bottom of that, what could be better to than to speak to the man himself?

She picked up the extension phone and carefully began to press the buttons.

'Grant residence; Steve Grant speaking.'

'Oh, hello, Steven. Ruby Watson here.'

'Hi, Auntie. What can I do for you?'

'Can you give me Tom Carson's phone number, please? I'd like to talk to him and there's no point in asking directory assistance for a number if he's with that Dixie person.'

'I can give you a cell phone number for her, but that won't help you find Tom. He's slipped through my fingers again, and Dixie thinks he's gone down East. Nova Scotia is my guess.'

'Nova Scotia! Whatever for?'

'That's where he was from, originally. I imagine he's still looking for his roots, or whatever one might call it after the shock he's had.'

'Oh, that is a nuisance!'

After a pause, Steven asked, 'Does Lys know you're doing this?'

Ruby gulped. 'Not exactly. It's just that she seems so distressed, and I do wish there was something I could do to help.'

'You mean she hasn't heard from the guy? I did try to insist that he call and put her in the picture, but I guess he didn't bother. Anyway, why would he take any notice of me? I'm just her brother!'

There was no more to be said. Ruby recognised the bitterness in his words and, after murmuring a few soothing platitudes, said her goodbyes and hung up. 'Now what, Ruby Watson? You mustn't fall at the first fence. Take it slowly, and try to come up with a plan.'

18

Tom Carson arrived in a small village some miles beyond Antigonish, bone-weary and with a day's growth of beard. It was a long time since he'd been home and there was nobody left here to welcome him. The lady in charge of the comfortable B&B assumed that he'd come to the area looking for his roots, and he did nothing to disabuse her of the idea. There was enough confusion in his mind as it was, without trying to explain his story to strangers.

If only Granny was still alive, his quest would be much simpler, but she had been gone for some years now. Her last resting place was a quiet country graveyard where tall pines overlooked the rows of ancient stones, and wildflowers grew at random along the pathways. His first task would be to buy a bunch of chrysanthemums to put on her grave.

'Never take roses to a grave,' she always said. 'A waste of money, they are, unless you're lucky enough to have a garden where you grow them yourself. Those hothouse things the florists sell cost the earth and they wilt in no time. Mums, though; you get your money's worth with them!'

So Tom chose sprays of chrysanthemums in a shade of deep maroon, turning down the florist's offer of baby's breath and some shiny green foliage.

'A spray of yellow mums would make a nice contrast,' the girl suggested, but he shook his head again. Granny hadn't cared much for anything in yellow.

'I know it's been a while since I was here,' he whispered, reverently laying his offering in front of her gravestone. 'I should have come sooner, but it's like you always used to say: life gets in the way. Anyway, I'm here now, and I hope there's some way you can hear me, Gran. I thought I had it all: a good job and the girl I hoped to spend the rest of my life with, but happiness seems to have slipped through my fingers. Everything's gone wrong and I'm here looking for answers.'

The only sound was the cawing of crows in the trees. Why did people visit cemeteries, he wondered? What could be gained by visiting the remains of loved ones? Granny had often said that she would be looking down from heaven to keep an eye on her family and if that were true, that was where she'd be, not here. Tom wasn't sure what he believed in that regard, but Eileen McGregor had been a church-goer and a firm believer all her days, and who was to say that she was mistaken?

'There are things I need to know, Gran,' he murmured, 'and I don't know where to begin. I suppose I could go to the church but I doubt if the same minister would be there after all this time, and written records wouldn't tell me much.'

He stopped, waiting, but now the only sound was the wind soughing in the pines. He sat back on his heels, looking around him. Evidently Decoration Day had been held here recently, for many of the stones bore arrangements of artificial flowers on top. One had a wreath of silk roses so skillfully made as to appear real. Roses. Rosebank! Something clicked into place in Tom's mind. Wasn't that the name of the old folks' home in the district? He had a vague recollection of his mother's membership in the Ladies' Auxiliary of the place, volunteers who visited the home to bring cheer into the lives of the retired men and women who spent their last years there.

Yes! A forgotten memory floated to the surface. Tom, an unwilling member of the high school glee club, going to Rosebank to perform Christmas carols for the residents. His voice had been in the process of breaking at the time, and the music teacher had made him stand in the back row, mouthing the words. He'd tried to wriggle out of the assignment but his parents had forced him to participate, saying that the old people were looking forward to the event and he mustn't let them down.

Now he knew what he had to do. He would go and question the residents, and with any luck there would be someone there who could set him on the right path. Not the same seniors who'd been there when he was a teen, of course — they'd be long gone — but surely somebody would be able to tell him something?

⋆ ⋆ ⋆

The administrator of Rosebank was most accommodating. Plump and cheerful, with pink cheeks and frizzy hair, she exuded warmth and an assurance that she cared about the people she looked after.

'I can't promise anything, of course,'

she said, 'but I'll do all I can to steer you in the right direction. If you can come back tomorrow evening I'll assemble everyone in the lounge. Then you can address general questions to the residents as a whole and make arrangements to speak to people individually later on.'

'What time should I come?'

'Not until after *Coronation Street* if you want anyone to come!' she said, laughing. 'They all have TV's in their rooms, of course, and when there is something they want to watch we can't get them out, short of shouting, 'Fire!'. We can't bully our people, you know, so you'll have to see them on their terms. It might help if you could tell them something thrilling, or startling, about your search. That would get them interested.'

'Sordid would be more like it,' Tom told himself mournfully. What were the choices? Either his kind, gentle father had had an affair when Tom was very young or, worse still, his mother had somehow been involved in something. Savagely kicking at a small rock that lay in his path, he wished that he'd never heard of Dixie Paulsen. If only the wretched girl had kept her distance for a few more weeks he'd have been in Australia, happily planning his future with Alyssa.

* * *

When Tom found himself facing an expectant crowd of seniors, his mouth went dry and it took him a moment to pull himself together.

'Get on with it, man!' a balding gentleman shouted. 'You haven't even got the projector set up, so what are you waiting for?'

'Excuse me?'

'The movie, man. It's supposed to be *The Guns of Navarone*.'

This brought others into the conversation. 'That's on Thursday, you fool! This is Tuesday, eh?'

'Are you doing genealogy, mister?

Best leave well alone, I say. There's no telling what might drop out of your family tree!'

'Especially when it's yours, Mac Livingstone!'

'Ladies and gentlemen, please!' The administrator stepped forward to quell the uproar. 'Mr Carson has come all the way from Toronto to speak to us, so let's give him a hearing, shall we? And no ribald remarks, Mr Lee. There are ladies present.'

Clearing his throat, Tom plunged into his carefully prepared speech. 'I've recently heard from a young woman who claims to be my half-sister. I don't think it's a scam, but you never can tell nowadays. The thing is, I don't see how that could be that we're related, and as my parents are dead I have nobody else to ask.'

He had their attention now. 'Why come to us, boy?'

'My grandma's family was from these parts. She's gone too, unfortunately, and Grandpa died before I was born.

I'm hoping that somebody here might remember Nan and provide me with a few clues.'

Many of those present remembered Eileen McGregor as one of the older girls when they were beginners at the school, and they had good things to say about her family. Good-living people. Hard-working. Always ready to give a hand to a neighbour. All that was reassuring, but it did nothing to further Tom's quest.

'I was wondering if my mother had an older sister?' he said in desperation. That could have been the answer — the old story of a young girl who fell pregnant and had to leave the area because of the shame, giving birth to her child in a home for wayward girls and giving it up for adoption. The baby had been Dixie, and for some reason her adoptive mother had lied about the circumstances. If that had happened in, say, the nineteen-fifties, it might be a possibility. But no, Dixie had been born in 1990, and even in backward places such dramas no longer took place. Single mothers were more likely to keep their offspring, settling down with them in accommodation provided by the taxpayer.

The rattle of teacups was heard and a woman in a green overall appeared, pushing a trolley containing a variety of sandwiches and small cakes. As one person the residents sat up straighter, craning their necks to see what the trolley held.

'I'm so sorry that we weren't able to help you,' the administrator said brightly, 'but you will stay for a cup of tea, won't you, Mr Carson?'

'Thank you, Mrs Brown,' Tom agreed, resisting the impulse to leave in a cloud of disappointment. Afterwards he was thankful that he'd stayed, for it was then that his big breakthrough came.

19

Aunt Ruby invited Ben to Sunday night dinner. 'You'll have to do the cooking, of course,' she told Alyssa, 'but I've plenty of pickles and relish that I put up last fall.'

'So what will we serve?' Alyssa joked. 'Dill pickle sandwiches?'

'How about a nice roast chicken with all the trimmings? I was thinking of mashed potato, gravy, green beans and corn niblets, with some of my secret-recipe stuffing. All enhanced with my dill pickles and beet relish!'

'I think I can cope with that. And what about dessert?'

'Pie, of course. You can't go far wrong with pie where men are concerned.'

'Lemon meringue?'

'No, no! You should serve something that'll stick to the lad's ribs. I suggest a nice apple pie, and maybe a cherry one as well. Let him have a choice. You'd better bring in a carton of vanilla ice cream to serve with it.'

So Alyssa spent a happy Saturday afternoon baking pies under Aunt Ruby's watchful eye.

'I'm glad to see you have a light hand with pastry,' Ruby said approvingly. 'I can't abide a pie crust that tastes like damp cardboard.'

'That's all due to my mother,' Alyssa told her. 'Her pies and cakes are as good as you'll ever find in a bakery. Dad says that if they ever fall on hard times she could go into the catering business. Everything I know about cooking I've learned from watching her at work.'

* * *

On Sunday afternoon Alyssa set the table using Ruby's best tablecloth and her 'for good' dishes. The silverware was shining and the glasses spotless.

Ginger ale was cooling in the fridge, and the coffee cups were waiting on the sideboard. All that was needed now was the arrival of the guest of honour.

Six o'clock came and went. 'What time did you ask him for?' Ruby asked, glancing up at the clock on the wall for the tenth time in as many minutes.

'I told him to come about six, because we'll be sitting down at six-thirty. Do you think I should start the potatoes now?'

'I guess so, dear. Oh, I do hope he won't be late. I find it so upsetting when people are late for meals.'

'Not to worry, Auntie. At least it's chicken, and that's just as good when it's cold.'

'Still!' Ruby grumbled. Alyssa hid a smile. She could imagine Ruby in her teaching days, chiding her small pupils for being tardy. Surely Ben would remember that, and arrive on time.

The sad notes of the mourning dove sounded from the bird clock on the wall, signifying seven o'clock. The two women exchanged glances.

'You don't suppose he's got the dates mixed, do you?' Ruby wondered. 'Perhaps he thinks he's supposed to come next Sunday, not today.'

'I don't know, Auntie. I think I'll call him on his cell phone, though, just to make sure.'

Moments later she looked up, frowning. 'That's odd. It went straight to voice mail.'

Ruby shrugged. 'Oh, well, I'm sure when we finally do hear from him he'll have a good explanation. He probably had to do overtime or something.'

'So why didn't he let us know?'

There was no answer to that, so when eight o'clock came, and there was still no word from Ben, they dished up the meal and waded through it in silence. 'When he does turn up we can make him a hot chicken sandwich,' Ruby suggested. 'There's plenty of gravy left for that, and of course there'll be pie to follow. Speaking of which, shall we have some now? Which would you prefer, cherry or apple?'

Alyssa shook her head. 'I seem to have lost my appetite, Auntie. Shall I cut you a piece?'

'No, thank you, dear. I must admit, I'm feeling rather concerned. Surely we should have heard something by now? If he hasn't shown up by nine o'clock I shall call the police station!'

'Oh, please don't. I'm sure that won't go down well at all. He's not supposed to get personal calls at work.'

'Nonsense, dear! I know the dispatcher, Amanda Greaves. I taught her in grade seven, and a right little madam she was, too. Many a time I sat there waiting when she was in detention, writing out lines. If she tries to give me a hard time I'll soon put her in her place, even if she is forty-five years old today!'

Was it Alyssa's imagination, or had the clock really slowed in its ticking? The minute hand inched its way around the clock face, passing the pictured blue jay, the cardinal, the tufted titmouse, and more.

'At times like this I do miss my knitting,' Ruby said with a sigh. 'And I can't get to grips with this silly crossword puzzle, either. What's a six-letter word for fortune, ending in 'e'?'

Alyssa shook her head. 'I've changed my mind. It's almost ten. Please go ahead and call the cop shop.'

'I will, dear, but no, I won't try to use that portable phone of yours. I just can't understand those things. I'll use my wall phone in the kitchen.'

When she returned her face was grey and drawn. 'I'm afraid it's bad news, dear. Ben has been in an accident and he's in hospital.'

'Not shot!'

'No, no. Something to do with a car chase, as far as I can make out.'

'But how is he? Is he badly hurt?'

'Amanda wouldn't say. She suggests that I ring back in the morning for an update.'

'Blow that! I'm going to call the hospital.'

'That won't do you any good, dear. You're not his next of kin.'

'Then who is? As far as I know he doesn't have any relatives in Beegrove. Why don't you phone, Auntie? Maybe the woman on the switchboard is another of your old pupils.'

'No such luck, dear. Well, I guess we'll have to wait and see. I'm for taking two aspirins and a cup of hot milk and going to bed. Why don't you do the same? Things always look better after a good night's sleep.'

But Alyssa wasn't to be comforted by any homespun remedies. 'I'm going to the hospital,' she announced as she fumbled in her purse for her car keys.

'All right, dear, if you must. But do drive carefully. Having you finishing up in the General is the last thing we need, and I don't know how I could explain things to your dear mother if that happened.'

* * *

Alyssa burst into the side entrance of the emergency department, having first gone to the main doors which, according to a notice, were locked for the night after ten p.m. Any activity that might be going on seemed to be happening behind closed doors, but at the far end of the reception area a woman sat alone in a walled enclosure. At Alyssa's approach she slid back a glass window and smiled encouragingly.

'May I have your blue hospital card, please?'

'What?'

'Your blue card, dear.'

'No, it's not for me. I mean, I'm not a patient.'

'Then how may I help you?'

Alyssa gulped. 'It's my fiancé,' she lied. 'He's had an accident, and I need to know if he was brought in here.'

'And your fiancé's name?'

'O'Hare. Ben O'Hare.'

'Well, I can tell you that he was admitted here, but I'm afraid you won't be allowed to see him. He's in the intensive care unit.'

'But that sounds serious! Can't you tell me what's wrong with him?'

'I'm sorry, but I'm not allowed to give out that sort of information.'

'Surely there's someone I can speak to! Isn't there a doctor here?'

'Dr Hansen is on duty in the emergency ward tonight. I'll page him and ask if he can spare you a few minutes. Why don't you take a seat in the waiting area, and someone will let you know when he's available.'

Feeling shaky, Alyssa did as she was told. She was the only person there, which must be unusual. The sound of an approaching siren interrupted her thoughts, and soon afterwards the entrance doors burst open and two paramedics thrust a loaded gurney inside. So much for speaking to Dr Hansen! Obviously the patients' needs took priority.

With one eye on the receptionist, Alyssa tiptoed towards the entrance and pressed the red button that caused the doors to slide apart. Leaning against the deserted ambulance, she waited for the paramedics to reappear. Perhaps they'd be able to tell her something, for even if they personally hadn't brought Ben here, they were probably aware of what had happened to him. Beegrove was a small, law-abiding place and, thankfully, there couldn't be all that many bad accidents and criminal activities.

Thoughts of Aunt Ruby and her war against rogue cyclists flashed through her mind. 'If the little brutes can't be made to drive responsibly on their bicycles,' Ruby kept muttering, 'what on earth will they be like when they get behind the wheel of a car? Why can't parents be made to understand that youngsters simply must be taught to act responsibly?'

Having come from the city, Alyssa well knew how many teenaged boys chose to steal a car to go joyriding in. Many times the vehicles were found abandoned some miles away and eventually returned to their distraught owners, but occasionally tragedy was the result. Was this what had happened here?

20

'What about Sarah Burton? I bet she'd know something. Why isn't she here, anyway?' A short man with a shiny bald head paused in his demolition of a large slice of chocolate cake.

'Who is Sarah Burton?' Tom experienced a frisson of hope.

'She is one of our residents,' Mrs Brown explained. 'I hadn't thought of her in connection with your problem, but Mr Fleming is quite correct. She does seem extremely knowledgeable about the people and history of the district. She wasn't well enough to come this evening, so she went to bed early with a sleeping pill. You'll just need to come back another time.'

'How about tomorrow?'

'I don't know. She has good days and bad days and, as I said, she wasn't well today. You might try right after lunch, before she has her nap. Who knows, she might be happy to see a visitor. But if she really isn't up to speaking to you, I'm afraid you'll have to leave her in peace, poor old soul.'

'I understand,' Tom said. He had no wish to upset the old lady, but on the other hand she might be his only chance to get to the bottom of things.

'I'll let her know you are coming, so she can be prepared,' Mrs Brown went on, 'but I really must warn you not to expect too much.'

* * *

Sarah Burton was an incredibly old person, or at least she seemed so to Tom. Her face was a mass of wrinkles, like an apple that has been in winter storage, and her white hair was sparse, showing expanses of pink skin underneath. She greeted him with waving hands and it was some minutes before he realised that she wanted him to hand her the glass containing her dentures.

'Can't talk right without my teeth,' she spluttered, when at last they were in place. 'Old age is a pest, young man. They fill us oldies with replacement parts, you know. That doctor wants me to get a new hip, but I told him, what's the point at my age? How old do you think I am, young man?'

'Eighty?' Tom suggested.

'Flatterer! I'll be ninety-seven next birthday, if I live to see it. What do you think of that, hey?'

'Remarkable. Now, about why I've come . . . '

'You want to know about your folks. Mrs Brown told me. Now then: who were they?'

'My grandmother was Eileen McGregor.'

'Ah, yes, I knew her. Soper, her name was, before she married Hugh McGregor. They had the two girls, both dead now. Which one was your Ma?'

'Maura.'

'Ah, yes. She was the pretty one. Clever at the school, she was, too. She should have gone for a nurse or a teacher, but no. She fell in love and married young, and what a mistake that turned out to be!'

Tom's heart skipped a beat. Perhaps they were getting somewhere now. 'Why was that, Mrs Burton?'

The old lady looked down at her swollen knuckles. 'I believe I won't say anything more on that score, young man. As my mother always said, if you can't say anything nice about a person, just say nothing at all.'

'Please, Mrs Burton, you can't stop there! I've come all this way to learn what I can about my background. I have an idea I was adopted as a baby, you see. I need to find out what happened.'

'Now you listen to me, young man! Sometimes it's best not to know these things. You look like you've done well in life; didn't Mrs Brown tell me you're a teacher in one of them fancy colleges back where you come from? Why spoil it all opening up a can of worms now?'

'Please, Mrs Burton. You said that my mother made a mistake. What did you mean by that?'

'Why, marrying your father, of course. He was a brute and a womanizer. Young women today, they wouldn't put up with the likes of that, but there was a time when marriage was for life. You did what you had to do to keep it going.'

'Oh, no, Mrs Burton; that can't be right. My father was the kindest man who ever lived. My mother adored him. The one thing that comforted me when they died in that car wreck was that they went together. If Mom had been left alone, I don't think she could have coped. No, no. You must be thinking of someone else, not Robert Carson.' Disappointed, he stood up, ready to take his leave. He had counted heavily on learning something from the old girl, but what could you expect of a woman who wasn't far off the century mark?

She shook her head at him as if he

was slow on the uptake. Her next words took his breath away.

'Robert Carson? Don't know nothing about him! I'm talking about your father, Andrew Paulsen.'

'What?'

'Your Ma's first husband, Andrew Paulsen. A nasty piece of work, if ever there was one. It was a lucky day for her when that brute took himself off. I never did know what happened to him. Somebody said he went out West, but maybe that was just talk. There must have been a divorce later, because after a while she married Carson. There was a time when poor Maura would have got the cold shoulder in these parts for a carry-on like that, but times are changing now, even in the back of beyond. Besides, none of it was her fault, poor soul, and she's at peace now. Have you been to see your grandma's grave? And poor Maura, wherever she's resting?'

'My parents were cremated, but I've been to visit Grandma.'

'I'll be joining her there soon, young man. Very soon.' Her voice trailed off and she seemed to have fallen asleep. Tom tiptoed from the room, his thoughts a jumble of relief and confusion. He marched through the double doors of Rosebank's main entrance, oblivious to the cry of the startled receptionist. He almost fell into his car and sat unmoving for a long time, trying to piece things together.

If the old lady had it straight, then he was indeed a half-brother of Dixie Paulsen. He had been born to Andrew Paulsen and Maura, and his birth father had abandoned them, eventually getting together with someone new and fathering Dixie. Paulsen must have left when his son was very young, for Tom had no memory of such a father figure. The only man in his life had been kindly Robert Carson.

'So I'm not adopted,' Tom decided, with a sense of relief. On the other hand he had taken Robert's name, so perhaps the man had formally adopted his wife's little boy. That was something different, and just one more example of what a kind and loving father Robert had been. What mattered to Tom was that Maura Carson was his birth mother!

There were, of course, other unsolved pieces of the puzzle. Mrs Burton had seemed to indicate that Andrew Paulsen had abandoned his wife and baby son, but that wasn't necessarily the case. If he was as unpleasant a person as she made out, it could have been Maura who had seen sense and shown him the door. Or had she fled from him, taking her little boy with her? That could explain why the Carsons had gone to live in Sydney, a place where Paulsen was unable to find them if he attempted to do so.

Tom gave a happy sigh. None of those details meant a hoot! He could now return to Mississauga to set his affairs in order. Dixie would have to be told what he had discovered, the tale watered down so as not to hurt her feelings. He would simply say that his birth parents had split up, a common enough occurrence in the nineteen-eighties.

More important than Dixie was Alyssa. Now that the mist had cleared he understood how much his attitude must have hurt her. Of course he should have told her about his hopes and fears, but somehow the shock of Dixie's arrival had made that impossible.

Even worse was the fact that, according to Steve, Alyssa had believed he'd betrayed her, practically on the eve of their wedding, with another woman. That was Steven's fault for jumping to conclusions, and presenting the gossip to his sister! Well, if Tom could persuade Alyssa that her brother was partly to blame, that should settle the whole matter.

21

'Hi there! Aren't you the gal who passed out on us when we attended that hostage situation?'

Alyssa, who had been leaning against the waiting ambulance, snapped to attention as the paramedics returned.

'Yeah,' she said, blushing. 'And I'm hoping you can tell me something about Constable Ben O'Hare. He was supposed to come to my aunt's place for dinner, but he never showed up. Then we heard he'd been hurt while on duty, and had been brought in here. Unfortunately the woman on the desk wouldn't tell me anything. She was going to let me speak to the doctor on duty but that didn't pan out, either. Who knows how long he'll be tied up with this new patient.'

'Can't tell you anything about that, ma'am. Patient confidentiality, you know.'

'But what about Ben?' Alyssa pleaded. 'Surely you can at least tell me what happened? That'll be all over the news by morning, so it can't be a secret. My aunt is very fond of Ben and she'll be out of her mind with worry if I can't reassure her. She's very elderly and not at all well.'

The second paramedic grinned. 'Is that Ruby Watson you're talking about? She's a game old bird! You couldn't kill her with a sledgehammer!'

'Don't tell me — she was your kindergarten teacher.'

He grinned again. 'Grade Two.'

Despite her anxiety, Alyssa had to chuckle. 'You don't know me. I can't think how you realised I'm staying with Aunt Ruby.'

'This is Beegrove, ma'am. Everyone knows everything, that's all.'

'Except that I don't know what happened to Ben!' Alyssa howled. 'If someone doesn't tell me something I shall scream!'

The first man took pity on her.

'There was an armed holdup at the Esso station. This fellow came in to gas up his truck and when he went inside to pay he held a gun on the attendant — who just happens to be my cousin Mary — and demanded the contents of the cash register. She gave it to him, of course, and he took off. Where he made his mistake was in not tying her up, so she called the cops before he was even out of the yard.'

'And Ben?'

'He was in one of the cruisers that gave chase. I was home at the time, looking out of my front porch, when I saw them going by, doing about a hundred and twenty clicks. I got the call soon after that to attend a pile-up on the highway.'

'Was anybody shot?'

'Nah. Seems the fellow hit a deer. He was so busy looking over his shoulder at the cops he didn't see where he was going. The cruisers piled into the back of the truck; going too fast to stop in time, I guess. Your Ben went through the windshield and got himself a concussion. He was conscious when we arrived but not making much sense. Cut about the face and hands from shattered glass, but nothing life-threatening. That's about it, ma'am.'

Alyssa realised she'd been holding her breath. She smiled wanly at the handsome paramedic. 'What happened to the robber?'

'Nothing much,' his partner assured her. 'Drunk as a skunk, so I guess he sort of bounced back when the collision occurred. He's in a nice cosy cell now, sleeping it off. His gun was just one of those replicas, so our Mary was never in any danger. Just as well she didn't take any chances, though. You never know with these idiots; one more trigger-happy than the next.'

Alyssa drove slowly back to Aunt Ruby's, still feeling shaken. She found her aunt pacing up and down, supporting her plaster cast with her left hand.

'It's all right, Auntie. He's okay.' Alyssa wanted to reassure the older woman right away.

'Thank goodness for that! Did you see him? Is he talking about what happened?'

'I gather he's in the ICU, just as a precaution, but other than that I didn't get a foot in the door. I did get the whole story from the paramedics, though, and a gorgeous hunk named Phil Markham says to tell you hi.'

'Phil Markham!' Aunt Ruby smiled reminiscently. 'And what a little devil he was! I had my work cut out with him, I can tell you. I'm proud to say that it's largely due to my hard work that he's an upstanding citizen today. And married with five children, too, so don't you be getting any ideas!'

* * *

Alyssa awoke the next morning, bleary-eyed. It had been almost four o'clock before she'd managed to drop off, and even then her sleep had been disturbed by nightmares. She stumbled downstairs to learn that Ruby had already phoned the hospital for news of Ben.

'Apparently they've moved him out of the ICU and into a regular ward. He can have visitors this afternoon, so we'll go in then, if he hasn't been released in the meantime.'

'Are you saying that you want to come with me?'

Ruby looked at her over the top of her glasses. 'And is there any reason why I shouldn't, miss? I've known him a lot longer than you have, you know. And my advice to you, young lady, for what's worth, is that you shouldn't wear your heart on your sleeve.'

Alyssa blinked. She wasn't in love with Ben O'Hare, was she? It might appear to anyone who didn't know her well that she'd been rushing around like a demented hen during the past few days, but that was because she counted him as a friend. And people cared about what happened to their friends, didn't they?

'What can we take him when we go?' she wondered, hoping to deflect more of Ruby's probing comments. 'We could stop at the market on the way and pick up some fruit.'

'I shall take a jar of my beet relish,' Ruby countered.

'What? You can't take pickled stuff to a hospital, Auntie.'

'I'm sure I don't know why not, my girl. In fact, I think anyone would be grateful. I've been in that place, remember, and their food is so bland a person might as well chew the newspaper.'

Alyssa couldn't decide whether Ruby was joking or not, so she changed the subject. 'I'll stop in at the gift shop and get him a Hershey bar with almonds,' she said. 'I know that's his favourite chocolate, and if he's too sick to eat it now he can always save it until later.'

* * *

They found Ben sitting propped up in bed, leafing through an ancient copy of

Maclean's Magazine. His face was a mass of scratches and gouges, liberally smeared with some sort of ointment.

'My goodness, you look like an illustration out of *National Geographic*,' Ruby told him cheerfully.

'What's that, Mrs Watson?'

'You know, one of those natives from a lost culture, with his face carved up into tribal symbols.'

'Gee, thanks, ma'am!'

'Seriously, though; how are you feeling? We heard you were concussed.'

'I have a headache, that's all. The worst part was getting a tetanus booster because of my face. I think I may be getting out of here later today, and then I'll be on sick leave for the rest of the week.'

'Every cloud has a silver lining!' Ruby said. 'But how will you manage, living alone as you do? I wonder . . . '

Alyssa stared at her in alarm. Surely Ruby wasn't about to volunteer her niece as a nurse-attendant? Or worse, invite Ben into her home for the duration? That would be going too far, too fast. Fortunately, whatever Ruby had been about to say was cut short as a white-coated technician popped into the room, brandishing a container full of ominous-looking vials and syringes.

'Just come to collect some of your blood, Constable O'Hare,' she told him. 'If you ladies wouldn't mind waiting out in the hallway?'

'Of course,' Ruby said. 'We should be on our way in any case. Come along, Alyssa; we must be going. We've done what we came for.'

Ruby seemed completely in command of the situation, yet moments later, when they were passing a waiting area, she suddenly fumbled her way to an armchair and sat down, clutching her stomach.

'Auntie! Are you all right? Shall I fetch a nurse? Would you like a glass of water?'

'No, no, dear. I'll be fine in a minute. Seeing poor Benjy there with his face all cut up made me realise what a dangerous job he has. It's not all arresting people for jaywalking and giving talks on personal safety to the Women's Institute, you know. He really could get himself killed, and I couldn't bear that, Alyssa. I simply couldn't bear that.'

'I know, Auntie, I know. But apart from driving recklessly he was never in any real danger, at least on this occasion. The gun wasn't real, you see. The robber couldn't have shot anyone.'

'No, not this time.' Ruby's face was grim. The world was a wicked place nowadays, even in Beegrove, and sometimes she longed for the placid world of her rural girlhood, when the worst that seemed to happen was when wolves attacked some distraught farmer's sheep.

* * *

Back at the house, Alyssa booted up her laptop, planning to email her mother. In a world that sometimes appeared to tilt on its axis, contact with her mother, who was happily vacationing in sunny Australia, gave her comfort. As a child she had gone to Anna Grant with her bruised knees or her broken dolls, and her mother had always known what to say or do. Perhaps we never completely outgrow the need for a mother's love.

Her heart seemed to leap into her mouth as she saw a message from her erstwhile fiancé. She was about to delete it, unread, when she managed to stop herself. She began to pace around the kitchen, not sure how to react to this unexpected contact.

'Something wrong?' Ruby asked.

'Oh, Auntie! You did make me jump! I didn't hear you coming downstairs.'

'It's these slippers,' Ruby said, pointing a foot to display fluffy pink footwear. 'Soft soles, you see. I can pad around like Felix the cat.'

'Email,' Alyssa said tersely. 'I've just had a bit of a shock.'

'Not one of those porn things, I hope? From some nasty person trying to get his jollies by preying on single women?'

'No, my spam detector stops most of those. This is a message from Tom.'

'Tom Carson?' Ruby asked, as if Alyssa might have a whole string of men named Tom trying to get in touch.

'Who else?'

'Well, go on then, child. Don't keep me in suspense. What does he have to say for himself?'

Alyssa sank down at the table, hiding her face in her hands. 'I don't know, and I don't think I want to find out. I'm trying to decide whether to just delete it without reading it.'

Ruby shot her an exasperated look. 'Oh, yes? And then the pair of us will never know what it was all about, and we'll be driven mad thinking up all kinds of scenarios. Go on, child! Get on with it!'

22

Tom found Dixie sprawled on the couch of her rented apartment, leafing through a movie magazine. Loud rock music bounced off the walls, and Tom was thankful that the downstairs neighbours were all at work; otherwise someone would be thumping on the ceiling with a broom.

'Can you turn that racket down a bit?' he bawled. 'I can't hear myself think!'

'Oh, you're back, are you?' Rolling off the couch, Dixie reached for the MP3 player. 'Did you find anything out? Are you satisfied now that I'm who I say I am?'

Unable to answer that, Tom opened the door of the fridge, staring gloomily at the contents. 'Don't we have anything in the place but bean sprouts and tofu? You might at least have gone to the grocery store.'

She shrugged. 'How was I supposed to know when you were coming back? You never said. Phone the pizza place if you're starving. And don't get anchovies; you know I hate them.'

Irritated, he called Domino's and ordered two pizzas. He didn't particularly like anchovies either, but an irrational desire not to let her bully him made him ask for them on his own meal. Dixie didn't seem to notice, just interrupting him to order extra cheese.

'So tell me everything,' she insisted, once they had eaten. She made no attempt to clear up after them, and it was Tom who collected the boxes and paper napkins and thrust them into the garbage container.

'Not much to tell, really. I didn't track down any documentary evidence, but I did talk to someone who had known my parents and your father.'

'It was a wasted trip, then?'

'Well, I was able to confirm that Andrew Paulsen was my birth father.'

Not that such evidence would stand up in a court of law, he thought, as Steve would no doubt confirm, but then Mrs Burton could hardly have picked the name out of the air.

With a sigh of satisfaction, Dixie made a remark that took Tom's breath away. 'That's good, then. Now we know for sure that we're brother and sister, we can make plans.'

'Plans? What sort of plans? Aren't you ready to head back out West?'

'Oh, I won't go back there, Tom. With Mom gone, there's nothing for me there. I'll stay with you, okay?'

Tom struggled to find the right words. 'Of course we'll stay in touch, Dixie, but I really think it's time I found another place of my own. Mind you, everything depends on how things go with Alyssa.'

'Alyssa! That's all in the past, isn't it? If she felt anything for you at all she'd have backed you up when you told her about us, instead of throwing her ring back at you. You're much better off without her. Tom and Dixie, two against the world, eh?' She lay back on the couch, doing cycling motions with her legs. Why couldn't she sit up and pay attention?

'Dixie. Listen to me. I'm glad we found each other; of course I am. But don't you think it's time we each went back to our own lives?'

She stopped pedalling and glared at him. 'Mom said you'd take care of me, Tom. That's why she wanted me to come and find you, if anything happened to her. Well, I'm in Mississauga now, and here's the plan. You go back to that fancy college of yours and make them give you your job back. We'll find a nice big apartment, and I'll keep house for you. It will be lovely; you'll see.'

'And what do you propose to do for money? Have you signed on for unemployment benefit, or started looking for work?'

'I can't sign on. I've never had a job, see.'

'Don't give me that, Dixie. You must at least have had summer jobs when you were a school kid, working in a corner store or delivering newspapers.'

She shook her head. 'I never did. Mom was always scared I'd get snatched by bad guys on the street, or killed in a hold-up. She thought if she could keep me at home I'd be safe.'

'Oh, yeah?'

'Don't give me that, Tom Paulsen. It's true. I swear.'

'Carson. My name is Carson.'

'Whatever.'

Something told Tom that continuing this line of talk was pointless, but he soldiered on anyway. 'What about when you left school? Didn't your mother want you to have a career?'

'I didn't have no qualifications. Besides, I had to stay home and look after her after she took sick, didn't I?'

And a fat lot of good you must have been to the poor woman, Tom thought, gazing around the untidy flat, but he didn't say it aloud. 'I'm going out for a walk. That pizza's sitting heavy in my stomach.'

'I told you to stay off the anchovies,' Dixie said, rolling over to pick up a paperback novel with a lurid cover. 'While you're out there, pick up a local paper. We should be looking at ads for apartments. A person has to be quick off the mark finding a place to live or everybody and his dog gets in ahead of you.'

Tom strode out of the flat, slamming the door behind him. He had to stand firm unless he wanted to have Dixie Paulsen hanging round his neck like an albatross. He was beginning to suspect that her motive in coming East had not been one of being reunited with a long-lost brother but rather in looking for a meal ticket. She had probably inherited that sense of entitlement from her father.

On the other hand, she was a twenty-two-year-old girl adrift in the world, and they were connected by blood. Didn't he owe her something?

She had presented him with an image of a dying woman, desperately trying to make provision for an only daughter after her death. How could he let her down?

She's feeding you a sob story for what she can get out of you, the cynical side of his brain told him. He kicked at an abandoned soda can, sending it spinning into the gutter. He made up his mind to leave her in the apartment while he went to sort out the muddle with Alyssa. The girl would be safe enough there for the time being, and perhaps he would get Alyssa to talk to her, and make her see sense. Yes, that was a plan.

* * *

'You want me to go to college?' Dixie said incredulously. 'And where am I supposed to find the money for that?'

Two days had passed, during which Tom had received no response to his emails to Alyssa. Feeling frustrated by his lack of progress, he decided to tackle his half-sister without further ado. She was a grown woman, after all; surely she could be steered into sensibly taking charge of her own life?

'Well, yes; I do think you could train for a career, Dixie. Is there anything in particular that interests you? Would you like to try nursing, let's say, or working with animals in a veterinary clinic? What about becoming a dental assistant?'

'Yuk!'

'Let's look at this another way, then. Where do you see yourself in five years from now?'

She looked animated for the first time. 'Nashville! I might be a famous country and western music star, making big bucks. What do you think about that, eh?'

Tom sighed. This girl made him feel as old as the hills. Had he been as foolish and naïve as this, just a few short years ago? Having dreams was one thing, but youngsters nowadays seemed to expect instant stardom, without having paid their dues. It was like signing up to run in the Boston marathon when you'd done nothing more strenuous than stumbling from the sofa to the fridge.

'So,' he began carefully, 'what have you done about it so far? Have you tried karaoke, for instance?'

She looked at him as if he were mad. 'That don't pay nothing. A mug's game, that is.'

And I know who's the mug here, Tom Carson! he chided himself. He took another deep breath. 'Look, Dixie, I know a lot of people trying to make it in the entertainment field and it's not easy. Very few of them can afford to chuck in the day job. The trick is to find some occupation that will pay the rent and put food on the table while they're waiting for that big break.'

Dixie pouted at him. 'You sound just like my mom! You old people are all the same. You don't believe in nothing!'

Tom had no answer to that. Not long

ago he had believed in a future with Alyssa, a dream honeymoon in Australia, and a secure job to return to as a college lecturer. All that had faded away when Dixie Paulsen arrived on the scene. If he were ever to get it back he had to act decisively. If Alyssa wouldn't return his calls and emails, he must go to this Beegrove place and talk to her in person. If that failed, he would have to find an apartment for himself and get some peace and quiet in which to map out his future. Dixie Paulsen was beginning to get on his nerves.

23

'Poor little Benjy!' Aunt Ruby sighed. 'It's dreadful to think of him lying there all alone in that dreary apartment!'

Alyssa tried to hide a smile. 'He's at home on sick leave, Auntie, not holed up in some dank dungeon. And anyway, how do you know that his place is dreary? Have you ever been there?'

'Of course I haven't, but I've seen a number of bachelor pads, and they're all the same. Unmade beds, sinks full of dirty dishes, and bathrooms with no toilet paper.'

'Really!' Having visited plenty of student accommodations in her time, Alyssa recognised the truth of this description but she had no idea how Ruby had come by the information. She was about to delve into this interesting subject when her aunt cut her short.

'So I've made up my mind, dear, that

one of us must go over there and help to relieve the poor boy's boredom.'

'And which of us might that be?'

Ruby did her best to look pathetic. 'Well, dear, I don't see how I could manage it, not with my poor arm. No, you can just whip up a nice chocolate sponge and off you go. If it makes you feel any better you can say I was worried about him, so I sent you to keep him company. In any case, he deserves a consolation prize after missing that lovely dinner you prepared for him on the evening he had his accident.'

Alyssa groaned. 'All right, then, but it will have to be a cake mix. I'm not good at doing baking from scratch and it would too bad if he got food poisoning on top of everything else.'

'Don't be silly, dear,' Ruby said, very much the stern schoolmistress. 'I'll leave you in peace now. It's time for my nap.' Alyssa's annoyance with the messages she'd received from Tom had not gone unnoticed by her great aunt.

Obviously the girl had no intention of getting back together with her erstwhile fiancé, so why should she continue to suffer from his unwanted attention? The sooner that something could be settled between Alyssa and Ben O'Hare, the better, and who better to play the role of fairy godmother than Ruby Watson?

* * *

Standing on Ben's doorstep, using one hand to ring the bell and the other to protect her gooey offering, Alyssa wished she'd worn something more attractive than frayed jeans and a faded tank top. She'd chosen these clothes in an effort to persuade herself that she was not coming here to impress the handsome cop, but now she felt scruffy and lacking in confidence.

The door flew open and Ben stood in front of her, looking sleepy. 'Oh, it's you!' he said, in charming greeting.

'I can go away again if you like,' Alyssa muttered. 'I've only come to deliver this cake, anyway. It's from Aunt Ruby.'

'Aw, did Mrs Watson bake me a cake? How kind; and her with a broken arm, too!'

Alyssa thrust the tin at him and stepped off the porch. 'There's no need to be sarcastic, Ben O'Hare! I'm sorry I came now!'

'Hey, hold up, woman! No need to be like that! Come ahead in and we'll take a look at this famous cake. I've coffee on the stove, and this is just what the doctor ordered.'

Reluctantly, Alyssa stepped inside. After a quick look around his kitchenette she nodded to herself. Yup! Aunt Ruby had been right.

'What's the matter?' Ben demanded. 'Seen a ghost, have you?'

'Um, no. I was just wondering if you were out of toilet paper, that's all.'

'What?'

'Never mind. It's just something Aunt Ruby said. Where's that coffee? I could do with a cup. I'm parched.'

Alyssa was pleased to see that apart from moving stiffly, and having a few cuts and bruises on his face and arms, Ben seemed none the worse for his accident.

'How long are you going to be off work?' she asked, sipping her drink appreciatively. Ben, concentrating on cutting himself a huge slab of chocolate cake, didn't answer immediately.

'I asked you . . . '

'I heard what you said, Alyssa. I have to see the doc again on Monday, and then we'll see. Why do you ask? Are you planning to come and read to the poor invalid?'

This puzzled her. Was he joking? She couldn't blame him if he was feeling cranky after the nasty shock of his accident, but why take it out on her?

'I'm only asking as a courtesy,' she said. 'Isn't that what people do when friends aren't well? Besides, that's the first thing Auntie will ask me when I get back to the house.'

'Friends, yes,' he muttered, not

meeting her eye. What was going on here?

'Ben, what is it? I didn't mean to upset you. Have I said or done something wrong?'

'It's nothing. Just forget it, will you?'

Alyssa sat up straighter in her chair. 'No, really. I insist. Tell me what's up and then I'll go away and leave you in peace, if that's what you want. I guess I shouldn't have come, but you know Aunt Ruby. She always has to know how things are with her little chicks.'

Ben laughed. 'Are you calling the lady a mother hen? She won't thank you for that!'

'Ben O'Hare! Just spit it out! I won't leave here until you do, so you may as well get on with it.'

He fiddled with the place mat on the table until Alyssa wanted to scream. In the background the wall clock ticked away, seeming to keep time with her heartbeat. Somewhere outside a child screamed in play, and a dog barked. At last Ben looked up.

'We've been out together a few times now, haven't we, Alyssa?'

'Yes, we have.'

'And we've had a nice time, haven't we? At least, I have.'

'Me too.' Good grief! Was he working up to a proposal of some kind?

'Well, then,' he muttered. 'The thing is, I thought we were friends, eh?'

'Well, of course we are.'

She waited. He picked away at the skin on the side of his thumb. 'I don't quite know how to put this, Alyssa. If I've given you the wrong impression, I'm sorry. I didn't mean to. I'm trying to say that I was happy for us to be friends, but nothing more than that.' He paused, reaching for the cake knife, which he used to scrape some excess frosting from the inside of the tin.

'Hey, look out, or you'll cut yourself!' Alyssa cried, as the blade bounced off the side of the tin after a particularly vicious jab. She was relieved when he put the knife down again, taking up a spoon instead. 'If you're worried that I might have got the wrong idea, you can forget that. I've enjoyed our friendship, too. Apart from Aunt Ruby, I don't know anyone in Beegrove, so it was good to have someone to go out and about with.'

'Oh.' Ben's mouth dropped open.

Alyssa almost laughed at the look on his face. He was like a little boy who has expected a scolding for some piece of mischief, only to find that it hasn't been forthcoming.

'It's just that you showed up at the hospital the minute you heard I was hurt, and now you've come here with this cake — which is very good, by the way! If you don't mind my saying so, it seems a bit, well, possessive.'

Keep calm, Alyssa told herself. *Be understanding!* She could examine her feelings of hurt and indignation after she left, which would be very soon, the way things were going.

'It is possible to be caring without being possessive, you know,' she said evenly. 'That's what women do, you know. I'm fond of you, Ben — as a friend — but I'm still in love with Tom Carson. I really have no room in my heart for anyone else in that way.'

Ben looked her in the eye at last. 'Sorry, Alyssa. I've made a fool of myself, haven't I? I guess I'm the same. I'm still in love with Clare, and I can't seem to move on from that.'

'Aunt Ruby told me that your fiancée had been killed in an accident, and I'm so sorry about that. I know there's nothing anyone can say that would help to ease the pain.'

Ben looked into the distance and there was silence for a while, broken only by the ticking of the clock. 'That's not all,' he said at last. 'I've never told anyone this, but you see, right before the accident, she broke off our engagement.'

'What?'

'She wanted me to give up police work, Alyssa. She said she couldn't stand the idea of waving goodbye to me in the mornings, knowing that it could be the last she'd see of me. I could be killed on the job, she said. Shot down by a drug-crazed gunman, or killed in a high-speed car chase. I told her that policing is my life, and I didn't want to give it up, even for her. When she stormed out of the apartment I let her go. I thought she'd come round in time. Instead she got behind the wheel of her car and drove off to her folks' place, right into the stupid, unnecessary accident that claimed her life.'

'Oh, Ben!'

'So now I'm the one who's had an accident, and you've rushed to my side like a ministering angel, and it's brought it all back, do you see? All I can think of is Clare and I don't think I can handle that right now.'

Alyssa nodded. Standing up, she patted him on the shoulder in a mute gesture of understanding. 'You can let Aunt Ruby have her cake tin back at some other time,' she murmured, for want of anything more meaningful to say.

Walking out to her car, she didn't know whether to laugh or to cry. Had she just been dumped, for the second time in a year? What were the odds against that?

24

Ruby stared at the young man on her doorstep. Not bad-looking at all, she decided, looking him up and down. Tall, rangy, black-haired. She might have fancied him in her younger days. It was a pity that his face was marred by such an anxious expression, though. It made him look like an unsuccessful door-to-door salesman, desperate to make his pitch. She felt a pang of regret that she was going to have to turn him down, but a teaching pension only went so far and she couldn't throw her money away on a whim. Besides, what was it the young people said? He might be playing the victim card as part of his scheme to unload whatever it was he was selling.

'I'm sorry, young man, but I don't buy at the door,' she told him. 'I can get everything I need at Wal-Mart.'

'Are you Mrs Watson? I'm Tom Carson. I was hoping to see Alyssa.'

Ruby's mouth formed an 'o' of surprise. 'Then you'd better come in, hadn't you? Although Alyssa isn't here at present, I'm afraid.' She stood aside to let him in, wondering what to do with the fellow now he was here. And why had she let him in without asking him for identification? Seniors were always being warned against letting strangers into their homes: unscrupulous scam artists who would rob them blind. But surely this young man was all right? How would a robber have known that Alyssa's fiancé — *ex-fiancé*, she corrected herself — how could he have known Tom's name? 'Stupid!' she said aloud.

'I beg your pardon?' The lad looked bewildered, as well he might!

'Oh, nothing; I was just thinking aloud,' she muttered. 'Do sit down, Mr Carson. Can I make you a cup of coffee while you're waiting for Alyssa? Or a glass of lemonade, perhaps?'

'Nothing for me, thank you. I stopped for too many coffees on the road. I'm sorry; I don't know who you are. Alyssa's aunt, I presume?'

Ruby held out her left hand. 'Ruby Watson, Mrs Sorry I can't shake hands properly. I'm a one-winged Winnie at the moment, I'm afraid. That's why she's here. Alyssa, I mean. Come to give an old lady a hand, no pun intended.' She was babbling. *Calm down, old girl!* She drew herself upright, favouring him with the stern look that had struck terror into so many mischievous children during her long teaching career.

'So, Mr Carson. Why are you here?'

'I've come to see Alyssa.'

'That is what you said, but what is it you want with her, young man?'

A glint of anger flashed in Tom Carson's eyes, quickly suppressed. 'With all due respect, ma'am, I think that's my business.'

'Is that so! Well, I have a stake in this, too. Alyssa is family, and families look out for each other. I think you should know that you've hurt that girl pretty badly, and I won't have any more of it, do you hear me? If you've come to make amends I'll make myself scarce while you say your piece to her, but if you've come to make trouble you can just turn around now and go head back to Mississauga!'

Tom stared at the feisty old lady, and then he began to laugh. 'Good grief! You remind me of a teacher we had in grade three. Mrs Harrison, her name was. Some of the teachers at Wesley Street School had trouble keeping order, but not Mrs Harrison! 'I want to be able to hear a pin drop,' she'd say when we'd been too rambunctious, and she had a real pin in her hand, too! She kept a few of them in the lapel of her blazer, all ready for action. Well, Mrs Watson, you don't need to drop any pins now, or any hints, either. I've come to make things right between me and Alyssa, so you've no need to worry about me upsetting her.'

Ruby nodded. Should she say anything about Alyssa's new relationship with Ben O'Hare, and her own hopes for their future together? But no; that was going too far. It was time to mind her own business; she had already said too much.

* * *

Alyssa had come in by the back door and so had missed seeing Tom's car beside the front sidewalk. Hearing the murmur of voices from the living room, she wondered who was visiting Ruby in her absence. Perhaps it was the minister, or someone from her aunt's bridge club? She'd just peep round the door to say hello, and then she'd make herself a cup of tea to take up to her bedroom. The unsatisfactory encounter with Ben had left her feeling bruised, and not a little annoyed.

'Darling!' Tom sprang to his feet and moved towards her with outstretched arms. Alyssa took a step backwards, dazed with shock.

'I think I'll just go and put the kettle on,' Ruby announced, but nobody heard her. She tiptoed out of the room, her heart beating fast.

Alyssa wriggled out of Tom's grasp, sinking down on the nearest chair. 'This is a surprise, Tom.'

'Yes, well, I had to come. You haven't been answering my emails, and my calls always go to voice mail. What else could I do? At least tell me you're glad to see me, Alyssa.'

Alyssa was unable to respond to this. So many conflicting emotions were whirling through her mind: hope, joy, hurt and anger. A month ago she would have given anything to find Tom on her doorstep, telling her that it had all been a horrible mistake, and that the wedding had to go on as planned. Now, though, too much time had gone by and too many things had happened.

'Well, say something!' Tom held out his hands towards her. She ignored the gesture.

'I didn't reply to your messages, Tom, because I thought there was nothing more to be said. I can't begin to explain how much you hurt me that day at Toronto Island. You really weren't making any sense, with all that stuff about needing to find yourself. And then I found out from Steve that you'd been seen around town with another woman, all lovey-dovey, apparently. Hardly the actions of a man in love with the woman he was engaged to marry.'

'But surely Steve explained all that! Dixie is my sister — well, half-sister — and meeting her came as a great shock to me, as you can imagine!'

'Yes, eventually, when you condescended to come clean with him.'

'So now you know the whole story, can't we make things right between us?'

Alyssa looked at him sadly. 'It's not as simple as that, Tom. There shouldn't be any important secrets between two people who were planning to spend the rest of their lives together, and this

Dixie thing is a big one. Why couldn't you have confided in me? It was too bad of you to leave me hanging like you did, wondering if I'd done something or said something to put you off.'

Tom's face flushed. 'Frankly, I thought you might have been a bit more sympathetic, Alyssa! Surely you see that I was shocked and confused! I needed space to work things out.'

'So you said, Tom.'

Out in the kitchen, Ruby winced at the sound of raised voices. She couldn't make out the actual words, but it was obvious that the conversation wasn't going well. Should she intervene with offers of tea and cookies? Or should she stay well out of it, and let matters come to a logical conclusion, no matter how unfortunate that might be? She was still dithering when the front door slammed, and after that the silence was broken by the sound of a car engine starting up. Darting into the living room she found her niece standing at the window, bleakly watching the departing car as it approached the end of the street.

'Stop!' she cried. 'Don't look!'

Alyssa turned to her in amazement. 'What, Auntie?'

'Don't you know, child? You must never watch a person until they're out of sight, or you'll never see them again. Everyone knows that!'

In other circumstances Alyssa might have laughed at this old piece of folk wisdom, dismissing it as a silly superstition. Now she was too saddened to rise to the bait.

'That's fine by me!' she said firmly, as she turned away. 'Just fine!'

25

'Perhaps it's just as well that it's all over between you and Tom,' Ruby said, deciding that a bit of reverse psychology was called for. 'If it wasn't meant to be, then surely it's just as well you found out now, rather than later.' Having received no response to this cliche, she took a deep breath before proceeding to Plan B.

'I'm so sorry that it's come to this, but now that it has, it does leave you free to get to know Ben a little better, and that has to be a good thing. As you know, dear, I . . . '

'No, Auntie; I'm afraid not. Are you suggesting that I have Ben to fall back on? I can't treat him like a sort of consolation prize. He's too nice a man for that.'

Ruby's grip tightened on her walking cane. She seemed to have put her foot in her mouth somehow. 'Not at all, dear. But both of you are free agents, and I thought . . . '

'Ben doesn't want to see me again. At least, I think that's what he said. He seems to think that I've been coming on too strongly, turning up at awkward moments as if we're already a couple.'

'Well, dear, you have to admit that you've rushed to his side in a panic on two occasions now, once at the hostage-taking and then when he was in that car accident.'

'I wasn't in a panic, as you put it!' Alyssa burst into tears. Horrified, Ruby leaned over and took the girl into her arms, somewhat handicapped by the cast on her right arm.

'There, there, dear! I'm sure that everything will be all right. He's just feeling a bit grumpy because of his injuries, I expect. And you know how men are; they can't deal with anything too sentimental. Once he's had time to think things over he'll realise that you only meant to show friendly concern.

After all, you have been seeing a lot of each other, so of course you'd be upset if he came to grief. Why, you'd feel the same about a woman friend, and I know that for a fact because you came all this way to help me out, an old woman you'd never met before!'

'There's a bit more to it than that,' Alyssa said, hunting through the pockets of her jeans for a tissue, and not finding one. Wordlessly, Ruby passed her a box of Kleenex.

'Ben told me something in confidence, Auntie. I guess it's no big secret, but swear you won't repeat it if I tell you. Ben mustn't ever know that you know.'

'Goodness me! Whatever is it?'

'You know that his fiancée was killed in a hunting accident?'

'Of course. I told you that myself.'

'It gets worse. She broke off their engagement because she thought police work was too dangerous. She wanted him to change careers, he refused, and they had a big row about it. She rushed off, into deadly danger. If they hadn't fallen out she would not have been in the wrong place at the wrong time. I think he probably blames himself, and now he wants to avoid getting into a similar situation with anyone else. I can tell that he really loves police work, Auntie, and doesn't want to change.'

'Nor should he,' Ruby said. 'And the world needs dedicated police officers like him. The trouble is I can see both sides of the argument, can't you? Being a policeman's wife can't be easy. Sometimes I think that our urban areas are becoming more and more like the Wild West every day. Drink, drugs and international crime cartels. I never dreamed that all that nastiness would ever come to a rural community like Beegrove, but here it is! There have been two horrible incidents in one summer, and our Ben is involved in both of them.'

'I think he'll have to find his own way through this muddle,' Alyssa said sadly. 'One thing is clear, and that is there's no future for Ben and me together, if indeed there ever was any chance of that. You see, Auntie, I love Tom Carson, and if I can't have him then I don't want any other man, even if I do get sidetracked for a while.'

Ruby leaned back in her seat, frowning. 'Then why on earth did you send the man away, child? He came all the way from Mississauga to try to put things right between you!'

'In a word, Dixie!'

'What?'

'Dixie, his half-sister. She's glommed onto him like a leech, and he can't break free.'

'Do leeches glom?' Ruby asked, momentarily diverted. 'I've often wondered where that expression comes from.'

'This one does! Apparently she's all alone in the world and now Tom feels responsible for her. I was just getting ready to forgive him for everything when he dropped a bombshell on me. He wants her to live with us after we're married. That just isn't what I had in mind when I fantasised about how married life with Tom would be. The next thing is, she'll want to be my bridesmaid, and I'm just not having that, Auntie. Maybe you'll think I'm selfish, but I can't help it. That's how I feel.'

'I read an interesting article when I was under the dryer at the beauty parlour,' Ruby remarked. 'It was all about the difficulties of living in blended families, as I believe they call them nowadays. That's when couples bring their children from previous relationships under one roof. You end up with step-siblings, half-siblings and all sorts of new problems. It's all about adjustment, the writer said.'

Alyssa shook her head vehemently. 'This is one thing I'm not going to adjust to, Auntie! If Tom had children, well, I'd do my best to be a good stepmother to them, of course I would. This Dixie is something else again. She's twenty-two years old and as far as

I can gather she's reasonably intelligent and in good health. She has to take command of her own life, just like the rest of us.'

'Hasn't she recently lost her mother, though? You can hardly blame her if she's all at sea. It does your Tom credit if he's ready to extend a helping hand.'

Alyssa got up and began to pace around the room. 'I'm quite willing to make friends with the girl and give her the moral support she needs. Help her find an apartment, and a job, and invite her over for meals from time to time. What I am not prepared to do is to have her move in with us, lying around the house all day like a lazy teenager, munching chips and watching soap operas while I go out to work to support her. As far as I can gather she's never held down a job, but has lived off her mother all these years. She simply has to get her act together.'

'And certainly she'll never be younger to learn,' Ruby said. 'It sounds to me as if you're prepared to go back to Tom if he agrees to all you've said?' she suggested.

'I suppose I might be. We didn't get the chance to discuss any of our other problems, because he was up on his high horse over that girl.'

'Then please pardon me for being an interfering old woman, but I do urge you not to pass up the chance of a reconciliation, Alyssa. Relationships are all about compromise, as I know only too well, and marriage calls for some give and take. Call him up, child, and start mending your fences, and do it fast. Will you do that for me?'

'I might.' Alyssa gave her aunt a half smile. There had been a time when she believed that she'd gladly crawl over hot coals to get to Tom Carson. Did she still feel that way? Reluctantly she admitted to herself that she did, although not without some concessions on his part. So would she make the next move? All right, she would, but not right away. Their disagreement had been pretty passionate. She must give Tom time to cool down first, or he was likely to give her short shrift, and then they'd be back where they started.

26

All was quiet when Tom reached the apartment where he'd been staying with his half-sister. Before leaving on his misguided trip to Beegrove he'd stopped in at the college and picked up some brochures and calendars for courses that he thought might interest Dixie. He hoped that she'd made a study of them while he was gone, although by the way she'd pouted when he'd thrust them into her hand that was doubtful. It also transpired that she had dropped out of high school before gaining any qualifications, which might mean her taking some make-up courses first, unless they would accept her as a mature student. Still, she had come to him, looking for help, so he would surely be able to guide her in the right direction.

He let himself into the apartment,

using his key. Not wishing to alarm her, he had first rung the bell, getting no answer, but he need not have worried, for the place was deserted. He looked around in disgust. Even by the standards of student accommodation in his youth, the place was a pigsty. Piles of dirty laundry had been carelessly thrown down in corners, and unwashed dishes were heaped in the sink. Empty beer cans littered the countertop.

If all that was bad enough, the state of the bathroom made him shudder. He closed the door in a hurry. Glancing into the two bedrooms he noted that both beds had been slept in, and the covers were thrown back as if the sleepers had got up for a moment, planning to return. It looked as if Dixie had been entertaining somebody, but who could it have been? As far as he knew she had no friends in Mississauga.

The living area bore traces of a number of meals. The boxes and foil containers held the remains of pizza and Chinese food. Somebody had been having a right old rave-up, but it was not his business. This was Dixie's apartment, and he had no right to criticise. One thing was certain: he was not going to roll up his sleeves and clean the place up!

He had brushed aside Alyssa's concerns when she'd balked at his suggestion that they invite his sister to share their future home, pointing out that they really didn't know the girl and it could be asking for trouble. He had naïvely assumed that Dixie, as the youngest member of the trio, would be pathetically eager to please, hanging on Alyssa's every word as First Lady in the home. Now he suspected it would be a recipe for trouble.

A key turned in the lock. 'Hello! Anybody home? Who is it? Who's in there?'

'It's all right, Dixie!' he called.

'Oh, it's you. You're back, then. Did you see Alice? What did she have to say for herself? Is she coming back to you, or what?'

'Alyssa. Her name is Alyssa.'

'Whatever.' Dixie sauntered into the room, hurling her leather jacket onto the couch as she passed by. 'So, what did she say? Are you back together?'

'We're working on it. Dixie, has somebody been staying here with you while I've been gone? I mean, the place looks a little — shall we say, lived in?'

'What if there is? I pay the rent, don't I?'

Tom was about to respond to this when the door opened again, and a large, unkempt man walked in. Dressed in a grubby T-shirt and khaki chinos, he boasted a prominent beer belly overhanging the worn leather belt that held up his sagging trousers. The hair that skimmed his beefy shoulders could do with a shampoo, Tom thought.

The vision spoke. 'Would this be lover boy, then?'

'Yeah,' Dixie replied. 'This is my brother, Tom, okay?'

The man stuck out a grubby hand. 'Pleased ter meet ya, fella. Alex

Paulsen, that's me.'

'Paulsen?' Tom's mouth felt dry. 'But I thought, I mean, aren't you dead? No, no, I can see you're not. Sorry, I don't know what I do mean!'

'I guess the girl hasn't told you about me, then. Fetch me a beer, will you, Dix? Ha, ha! We got you going for a minute there, didn't we, boy? You thought I was your old man, back from the dead, didn't you? No such luck. I'm his cousin, Alexander the Great, understand?'

'I guess so. I don't know anything about the Paulsens, other than that your cousin Andrew was married to my mom at one time.'

'Steady on there, fella! That's your dad you're talking about. You don't remember much about him, I suppose, on account of your folks split up when you were just a wee lad. Well, come on and sit right down and I'll tell you everything you want to know.'

There wasn't anything that Tom wanted to know — he had found out far too much already — but he sat down and prepared to be informed. 'I suppose you've known Dixie here all her life,' he murmured.

'Off and on. That's when I wasn't doing time.'

'Time?' Tom said faintly.

'You know, as a guest of the state. Not that I ever did anything really bad, you know, but a guy has to make a living the best he knows how, and some folks don't like that. Well, I just got released the last time and I went to see how Nellie was doing — that's Dixie's Mom — and just as I got there they took the poor woman into the hospital and she never came out. Well then, I said to Dixie here, let's you and me go look up this brother of yours, the fancy university professor, and see what he can do for us. I bet he's living off the fat of the land in a big fancy house and he'd just love to have us come and visit. Blood is thicker than water, eh?'

'I thought this was your mother's

idea, Dixie?' Tom turned to the girl, indignation oozing out of every pore.

'So it was. Him and her, they both had the same idea. So I said, why not? I didn't have nothing else to do.' The pair of them looked at Tom expectantly.

'Well, I'm sorry to disappoint you,' he told them, 'but I have nothing to offer you. I've given up my job, and my savings are all spoken for. I'm leaving for Australia very shortly, and as a newcomer I shan't be able to get much of a job when I do get there.'

This of course was an exaggeration, but Tom had no wish to anger the pair. Alex Paulsen was overweight and flabby, but he had great hams of hands that looked as if he could do anyone a mischief, and he was parked between Tom and the door.

'I told you he wouldn't fall for it!' Dixie said angrily. 'Well, then, Tom Carson, or whatever your name is, if you don't mean to help us, get out of my apartment. I sure don't want you here!'

'Gladly,' Tom said. 'I'll just collect my things and then I'll be out of your hair.'

* * *

Far from having a 'big, fancy house' Tom was temporarily homeless. With no wish to spend the night in his car, he drove to the Grants' house, where he found Steven hard at work on his studies.

'It's okay, I was ready for a break,' Steven told him. 'I've read this page at least six times and nothing seems to sink in. Have you eaten? I could make you a sandwich, or we could send out for something.'

It seemed an age since Tom had stopped on the road for breakfast. While Steven slapped soya margarine on rye bread, and hunted in the fridge for cold cuts and mustard, he told his sorry tale. 'I feel such a fool,' he concluded. 'I fell for Dixie's story hook, line and sinker.'

'Don't feel bad. You weren't to know

she's a con artist, and it sounds like that uncle of hers talked her into it.'

'Cousin.'

'Whatever. Now tell me, how did you make out in Beegrove? Are you and Alyssa back together? When is she coming home?'

'Whoa! One question at a time, please. About Alyssa and me? Sadly, I'm no further ahead on that score. Just as I was beginning to make headway she got started on the subject of Dixie coming to live with us — or not, as the case may be — and then it all fell apart.'

'At least that's no longer an issue,' Steven said, cutting the sandwiches in two. 'You want a pickle with that? We have Polish dills, nice and juicy, or pickled cabbage.'

Tom's mouth watered.

* * *

Much later, sprawled restlessly in Alyssa's bed, Tom reviewed the events of the day. Alyssa's spirit seemed to inhabit this room still, filed as it was with all the treasures of her childhood. The Nancy Drew books on the shelf, the pop posters attached to the walls, even Travis, the tattered teddy bear on the pillow, all reminded him of their owner, now grown up and gone. Piles of boxes apparently held items she'd brought here from the apartment she'd given up in preparation for their trip to Australia.

He groaned. How could everything have gone so wrong? He winced when the memory of their breakup replayed itself in his tired brain. How she had torn his ring from her finger before stomping off. There had been no need for her to do that; no need at all. Surely what he'd asked of her had not been so unreasonable? The shock of learning about his true parentage had been great, and he'd known that he couldn't settle until he'd got to the bottom of it all. And he'd been right to act as he did, because his trip to Nova Scotia had set his mind at rest.

He'd attempted to explain that to Alyssa, but she hadn't tried to understand. 'Blended families are the norm nowadays,' she'd insisted, although when it came to taking his half-sister into the fold she'd been less accommodating.

In a half-forgotten memory from his boyhood he heard his grandmother talking about some neighbour who had upset the other women at the church missionary society. 'She wants to rule the roost, that one, and we're not having it! I pity that poor man of hers. A hen-pecked husband if ever I saw one.'

The child hadn't understood. 'What's it mean, Grandma? Mrs Morton isn't a hen!'

'It means she wants to wear the trousers, that's what. Now, you go and play nicely with your truck while I get this stew on the stove, or we'll get no dinner today.'

He still hadn't understood, for didn't

every woman they knew wear trousers? The only time his grandma changed into a skirt was on Sunday when they went to church. Now he wondered about Alyssa. Was it possible that she was one of those bossy women who always had to have her own way? Perhaps he shouldn't be too quick to go back to her, cap in hand, in case he appeared to be a pushover. Yes, he might bide his time and see if she made the first move.

27

Ruby felt heartbroken on Alyssa's behalf. The poor girl wore a wan expression and the tip of her nose was all red, as if she was fighting off a cold. Passing the door of the guestroom in the night, on her way back from the toilet, Ruby could hear muffled sobbing coming from inside. Whatever she might say to the contrary, it was obvious that the girl was still desperately in love with Tom Carson, and not about to recover from that state. What a pair of young fools! Ruby wanted to bang their heads together and lecture them on the folly of wasting precious time over things that didn't really matter. As far as she could see they were both stubbornly refusing to consider the other's point of view, and that was no good at all.

Carefully removing her dentures and placing them in the glass on the bedside table, she then thought about poor Ben. There was another one who was suffering the consequences of misguided thinking. She had regretfully given up the idea of getting him married off to Alyssa, but that didn't mean that the two of them couldn't be friends. She would have to see what she could do to bring that about.

* * *

At last Ruby was able to get rid of the cast on her arm. Alyssa drove her to the hospital, where they had a lengthy wait before their turn came. The waiting room was filled with a mixture of people, many of whom were waiting for appointments at the various clinics, where visiting consultants from the city held sway.

A play area at the end of the hall was overrun with squabbling children, and one of these, a boy of about five years old, trotted up to Ruby, staring at her plaster cast.

'Why do have that thing on your arm, lady? You look stupid.'

Alyssa noted with alarm that the light of battle had come into Ruby's eyes.

'I broke my arm, and the doctor put this on to help it mend.'

'How did you break your arm?'

'I did it when I was kick-boxing.'

'Eew! Then how come you broke your arm, and not your leg?'

'Because I've only got two legs, and I need both of them to walk on.'

Apparently satisfied with this, the child ran back to the toy box, where he snatched a small car from a toddler, who started to scream.

'Kick-boxing, Auntie!' Alyssa hissed, under cover of the noise. 'Do you really think you should tell tall stories like that? I'm sure that boy believed you.'

'I was being ironic, dear. There's nothing wrong with that. Beside, that child was rude, calling an elderly person stupid. If I'd told him what I really thought, he'd have taken a severe blow to his self-esteem. He should learn to respect his elders!'

Alyssa nodded, her mind elsewhere. But her aunt sat up a little straighter in her institutional armchair and mulled over what had just happened. What with Alyssa's problems and her own injury, she had become sidetracked from her mission of teaching better manners to the young, but now she must get back on track. And, if in so doing she could help Alyssa and her young men, so much the better!

* * *

'You've healed very nicely, Mrs Watson,' the young doctor told her, when the cast had been removed and an x-ray taken. 'Of course, you won't be doing any push-ups or weight lifting yet awhile, but with a few sessions of physiotherapy you should be able to take part in the activities you enjoy — knitting, or water-colour painting, and that sort of thing.'

Ruby smiled. 'And I promise to stay off ladders from now on, Doctor.'

'See that you do! I don't want to see you back here again.'

What a nice young man, Ruby thought. *Even though he's busy, he can still find time for a bit of a joke. I bet he didn't tell old ladies they were stupid when he was little more than a toddler. He was obviously very well brought up.*

'There you are!' Alyssa said, smiling. 'All finished, and ready to go home? Do you want to make any stops along the way?'

'I thought we could go to that Splasharama place, if that's all right with you.'

'What?'

'It's one of those paintball places, dear. People go there and try to cover other people in paint, although goodness knows why they should want to.'

'You're not serious, Auntie!'

'No, no, dear, of course not. I was just being ironic again. What I really want is to go home and put my feet up with a nice cup of Earl Grey. Hanging around in that place has made me quite thirsty.'

* * *

Later, when they were waiting for the kettle to boil, Alyssa decided that the time had come to share her plans with Aunt Ruby. 'There's something I've been meaning to tell you, Auntie,' she said, as she cut open a packet of chocolate digestives.

'Yes, dear?'

'Well, I've been thinking. I've loved being here, and I hope I can come back for a visit some other time, but now I think it's time I was moving on, don't you?'

'I don't know what to say, dear. It's been wonderful of you to have stayed so long with a poor old lady, and I've loved having you here. I can't imagine what I'd have done without you. They'd have given me meals on wheels, I expect, and a couple of hours a week of what they call personal assistance, but it would not have been the same at all. I very much appreciate all you've done, I can assure you of that. Still, I realise that you have your own life to live. Where do you mean to go?'

Alyssa hesitated. 'Australia, I think. I haven't seen mom and dad for ages, and they'll be leaving Australia soon on the next stage of their adventure. Now's my chance to see that country while I still have a fixed destination to go to.'

'Won't it be upsetting for you, dear?' Ruby didn't want to spell it out, but surely it would be painful for the girl to go there now that her wedding plans had fallen through?

Alyssa smiled bravely. 'I'll survive. If I'm going to travel at all, now's the time, because if I stay in Canada I'll have to think about finding a job and a place to stay.'

'You know you're most welcome to stay on here, dear.'

'I know, and I love you for suggesting it, but I have to get my act together somehow. Yes, I'll go and see my parents, and after that, well, I'll see what I might like to do next. I plan to email Mom tonight and see what we can come up with. Meanwhile, I will stay on here for a little while, if you don't mind, just to see you through the physio and so on. I don't suppose you'll feel up to lifting heavy saucepans, for a start.'

* * *

Ruby had some thinking to do. The girl was being very brave and sensible, of course, and obviously her parents were the right people to provide advice about the future. But was she being too sensible? What had happened to the power of romance? Back in her day young women had fantasised about giving up everything for love, of winning the men of their dreams and fighting to keep them. Of course there had been a war on then and emotions were heightened. If you knew that your young man might be killed at any moment, of course every hour spent with him seemed precious.

All right, so Alyssa was going to Australia. That didn't mean that she'd necessarily be cut off from everyone in Canada for the rest of her life. If things worked out for Alyssa and Tom, he could always follow her there in due course. Come to that, so might Ben. They must have police officers in Australia.

28

Anna Grant was delighted to learn that her daughter was planning to join them in Australia. 'You'll love it here!' she enthused. 'It's a wonderful country, and we were planning to stay on longer than we originally thought, because there is so much to see and do here. And there's really no need for you to rush back in search of a job. We can well afford to have you stay with us for a good long break. You might even consider coming with us when we visit New Zealand, but we can discuss all that when you come.'

'Sounds good,' Alyssa emailed back. This was an opportunity not to be missed, and she could afford to do it. She had saved long and hard for her wedding, and as that was not now going to take place, why shouldn't she splurge on a lovely long holiday? She had earned it.

'Is there anything you need from the house that I could bring over with me?' she asked.

'Well, with summer coming here I would like that white sleeveless blouse of mine — you know, the one with the pink flowers on the pocket. It should be hanging in my walk-in closet. And why don't you take some snaps of Pookie and Rybena? I do miss them. Is Steven looking after them properly? I hope they haven't been pining for me. And please remind Steven to take them to the vet soon, for their rabies boosters.'

Alyssa contacted her brother immediately. 'I'll be coming home in about two weeks, I should think. Don't tell Tom! And Mom wants to know if you've taken the pets to the vet for their shots.'

A reply came back immediately. 'Of course I did! She's been on my case about it for weeks! And I won't need to tell Tom anything, because you'll see each other when you come. He's been staying at the house, mooning about in your room with a face like a wet weekend.'

Well, of all the nerve! She couldn't bear the thought of him sleeping in her bed and possibly rummaging through her things, even if it hadn't exactly been her room for quite some time. If they weren't meant to be together, why couldn't they have a clean break?

The phone rang, interrupting her thoughts. The call was on Aunt Ruby's landline so it was probably from one of her cronies at church, or the bridge club. They could ring again later, whoever they were. If Alyssa answered it now it would only be to say that her aunt had gone to the shops, and there was no telling when she might be back.

The phone continued to ring until at last, exasperated, Alyssa snatched up the receiver. 'Yes?' she barked.

'Oh, there you are, dear! Thank goodness! I was afraid you'd gone out, and I'm in such trouble!' The voice on the line quavered and stopped short.

'Aunt Ruby! Is that you? Where are you? Are you hurt?'

There was a long silence, and then Ruby said in a small voice, 'I'm at the police station, dear. Can you come and bail me out?'

'What?' Alyssa looked at the receiver in disbelief.

'Are you there, Alyssa? Please come! I need you!'

'Auntie! Please tell me what's happening. I can't understand this at all.'

A new voice came on the line. With a pang, Alyssa recognised Ben's pleasant tones. 'I'm afraid your aunt is in a bit of trouble. Can you come on down? I'll explain everything when you get here.'

Alyssa gulped. 'Should I get hold of a lawyer?'

Ben laughed. 'Oh, I don't think we need to go that far. She's not exactly under arrest, although she may be charged with mischief.'

What had the woman been up to now? Alyssa wondered, as she splashed water on her face and ran a comb through her hair, readying herself for driving the short distance to the police station. Had she been picketing Main Street carrying a banner complaining about the rudeness of modern youth? But that was highly unlikely, for when she'd left home that morning she'd taken nothing with her but a raffia shopping bag. Alyssa had watched her putting her small leather purse inside it and a spare cardigan 'in case the weather turns chilly'.

At the police station she was shown into a small interview room where she discovered her aunt sitting at a table, quietly sipping a cup of tea. Was that a smug expression on her face? Alyssa had been expecting a chastened look. She slid into a chair beside her aunt, glancing up when Ben entered the room, closing the door behind him.

'Gidday, Alyssa. How are ya?'

'I'm fine, thanks! But what's all this about? Auntie, what have you done?'

Ruby shrugged. 'I may as well let him tell you. He seems to have it all in hand.'

Ben joined them at the table. 'It seems that Mrs Watson here has been shooting people in the street. She had a water pistol — which has now been confiscated as evidence — filled with a red substance and she nailed Mayor Brunhofer right on his good white shirt!' He grinned at Alyssa, who was not amused.

'Surely there must be some mistake!' she snapped.

'I'm afraid not.' He bent over and lifted Ruby's right hand, which was stained with a crimson substance. 'See this? Caught red-handed, if you'll excuse the cliché.'

Alyssa groaned. 'So what happens next? Do I really have to pay bail?'

'That won't be necessary. Just take her home and keep an eye on her. If she's required to make a court appearance somebody will be in touch.'

'I'm so glad that you and Ben are on

speaking terms again,' Ruby said chirpily.

'Please don't tell me you did whatever it is you've done just to get us back together, Auntie? Not that we ever were together, exactly. No, don't tell me anything more right now. I'm a bit shaken up and I need to concentrate on my driving. Wait until we get home and you can explain yourself over a nice cup of tea. All right?'

'Not tea, dear. I'm awash with tea already.'

Gritting her teeth, Alyssa drove on in silence. What she needed was a stiff drink, but since her aunt wouldn't have liquor in the house, she wasn't likely to get one. She would make coffee — good, strong coffee!

* * *

'I'm sick and tired of children and youths speeding up and down the sidewalks on bicycles, putting senior citizens at risk,' Ruby said when they she was comfortably ensconced in her rocking chair, moving gently.

'I know you are, Auntie. You've said so, many times.'

'Yes, well, why isn't anything being done about it? The police can't do anything. As Ben says, they have to catch them in the act but the young devils are too wily for that. So I thought I'd shoot them with red ink and that would be the proof we need, do you see? The officers would give them a good talking-to, we might get some publicity for our cause, and Main Street would be safer for everyone.'

'That doesn't look like ink to me.' Alyssa stared pointedly at Ruby's right hand.

'Well, no. They don't seem to make it any more. I tried ketchup, but it was too thick and it gummed up the pistol. I really would have loved one of those paintball guns, but I decided that might be going too far. Besides, I didn't know how to get hold of one.'

'Don't keep me in suspense, Auntie.

What did you use in the end?'

'Beetroot juice!' Ruby said triumphantly. 'I opened a jar of those pickles I made before I had my accident and there it was! A nice bright colour, and a thin enough liquid to use in the water pistol.'

'And leaving an awful stain behind it!' Alyssa said, her expression grim. 'I remember helping Mom to put up beets and accidentally splashing juice on my nice white T-shirt. It couldn't have been more permanent if I'd tie-dyed the thing. Oh, Auntie, the mayor's shirt! What a disaster. He'll never get it clean.'

'I know, and I'm sorry about that. I shall offer to replace it, of course.'

'But why did you target him, of all people? Did you want him to stand up in council and pass a by-law or something?'

'Oh, that was an accident. This child came pedalling along and Brunhofer had to jump aside to avoid being hit. I fired my pistol but my hand was too shaky and it spoiled my aim. I guess my wrist isn't back to full strength yet. Anyway, instead of getting the boy I hit the mayor by mistake. He threw a hissy fit and some officious woman called 911 on her mobile phone. I was quite pleased at the time because I thought they'd deal with the boy, but instead they tried to make out that I was at fault. Imagine!'

'But oh, what if the Mayor presses charges and you have to go to court?'

'Let him! It's about time that the council did something about this situation. And what can they do to me, anyway? The magistrate will let me off with a caution, I expect.'

'Or he might recommend sending you to a mental institution, Ruby Watson.'

'Balderdash! When they're releasing so many of the inmates 'back into the community' as they put it? People who have nowhere to go, and nobody to care about them? That's another disgrace, if you ask me!'

Defeated, Alyssa let her aunt ramble on. With any luck the presiding magistrate would be yet another of Ruby's former pupils. She certainly seemed to have the population of Beegrove in her pocket.

The doorbell rang. Alyssa went to answer it, frowning at the skinny young man dressed in corduroys and a tattersall shirt who stood on the doorstep, chewing on a wad of gum.

'Yes? Can I help you?'

'Jason Finch, *Beegrove Chronicle.* I'm here to follow up the story of pubic mischief on Main Street.'

Alyssa was about to slam the door on him when Aunt Ruby's dulcet tones were heard.

'Is that you, Jason Finch? Come away in!'

Sighing, Alyssa stood aside to let the reporter in.

29

'Just look at this!' Ruby chortled. 'I've made the front page of *The Chronicle!*'

'It must be a slow week for news,' Alyssa muttered. It was hardly the sort of stuff that the big Toronto daily, the *Globe & Mail,* would print. The little paper was printed in the town but distributed over a wide area of the surrounding countryside, arriving in people's roadside mailboxes by courtesy of a grey-haired lady driving a Toyota truck.

'This is human interest,' Ruby told her. 'Local papers don't care much about the state of the economy or uprisings somewhere across the world. We like to know about who grew the tomato resembling the prime minister, or who spotted the first robin of the season. And just look at this fine picture of me! All my former pupils will see that and be made aware of my campaign!' She clipped out the piece while Alyssa peered over her shoulder at the headline. In large black type it read, *Beegrove Senior Targets Mayor.*

'According to you, that's not true,' Alyssa exclaimed. 'He just happened to get in the way when you fired your water pistol.'

'Ah, but if you read on, you'll see that I'm quoted as saying that Brunhofer and his cronies should do more to protect us seniors. After all, we have the vote, just like everyone else, so they should listen to what we have to say. I may not have deliberately sprayed the man with beetroot juice, but I've certainly challenged him to do something about the problem of crazed youngsters on bicycles.'

Alyssa looked up at the ceiling. She supposed that no real harm had been done. It had all been a storm in a teacup, as her grandmother used to say. Let Aunt Ruby have her fifteen minutes of fame and then all the fuss would die down.

* * *

When Alyssa answered her mobile phone the next day she was none too pleased to hear Tom's voice at the other end. 'How did you get through to me?' she demanded.

'By using Steve's phone. I knew you wouldn't pick up if you thought it was me. No, wait! Don't hang up! This is important. Have you seen the CBC news website today?'

'No, I haven't had a minute. What's up that's so important?'

'Never mind. Just go and take a look!'

Alyssa glanced over the website, which had the usual mix of national and international news and sports. She groaned when she came to the Offbeat section and saw the headline, *Granny Get Your Gun*. It was a colourful account of Ruby Watson's one-woman crusade to sort out the youth of Beegrove, Ontario. The piece was accompanied by a particularly unflattering photo of Ruby standing on her doorstep with her white hair flying in all directions.

'What have you got there, dear? Anything interesting?'

Alyssa jumped. 'I didn't hear you creeping up on me like that! As it happens, it's you, in glowing technicolour!'

'Ouch! That nasty little papa-whatever-you-call'um leapt out at me when I stepped out to pick up the mail yesterday. Do I really look like that?'

Alyssa tactfully ignored the question. 'Look, you're listed in the Most Commented section.'

'What might that be, dear?'

'It's where people can post comments on the news stories of the day.'

'Oh, yes? What do they say about me, then?'

Alyssa read off some of the comments while Ruby listened, smiling broadly. Many people commended her for taking a stand, saying that young people today had no manners and were allowed to run wild. Something had to be done, or children would be ruling the world before long, if they weren't already. If people in positions of authority couldn't act in the pubic interest, then thank goodness for Ruby Watson! Several people mentioned their own experiences of being roughly shoved aside or narrowly escaping being hit by bicycles.

'Good! Good!' Ruby chortled, rubbing her hands together in glee. 'This should get things moving! I do object to being referred to as a granny, though. How rude! Sadly, I never had children. I did so want to have a little girl or boy of my own, but it wasn't to be. It was fortunate that I had my pupils to love and guide.'

'Unfortunately not all these posts are complimentary,' Alyssa said. 'Here's one that calls you a senile old biddy. And someone who signs herself 'A

Mother in Midland' maintains that you've set a poor example to the children of Canada by throwing dirt at an elected official.'

'Phooey! If the youngsters have noticed anything at all they'll get the message that we should stand up against injustice! And anyway, it wasn't dirt. It was honest-to-goodness vegetable juice!'

While Ruby was jubilant at the uproar her action had created, Alyssa was somewhat disturbed. There were a lot of crazy people out there, and who knew what might happen? They could get a brick thrown through the window, or worse. Suddenly she felt very much alone.

When Ruby had gone to have a bath, Alyssa emailed her brother. 'Can you come and stay for a day or two? Just until Auntie's court appearance is over? She's quite chipper about the whole business, and she doesn't realise what she may have started. I'd feel happier if we had some male protection, and it shouldn't put you out too much. You can bring your books with you and do your studying here.'

'Male protection!' Steven replied. 'Whatever happened to my feminist sister? Okay, Lys; I'll see what I can do.'

* * *

The summons to appear before the magistrates came in the mail. In due course Ruby and Alyssa set out for the county courthouse, ready for battle.

'I wonder how I should act,' Ruby mused, having tried on and discarded one hat after another, finally settling on an inoffensive navy blue felt. 'Should I appear belligerent, or contrite? What do you think dear?'

'I think you should keep a low profile, Auntie. No doubt you'll get a scolding, but don't you answer back! Yes sir, no sir, three bags full, sir! You don't want to put his back up, or heaven knows where that might lead.'

'I thought I might look pitiful and

blame everything on my advanced age,' Ruby told her, grinning roguishly.

'I wouldn't do that if I were you. They might even refer you for psychiatric assessment, and then where would you be? Just keep your cool, and with any luck it will all blow over.'

* * *

By the look of the assembled crowd the court had a full docket, although it was hard to know how many of the people were mere spectators. The press gallery was full, and Alyssa had a nasty idea that Aunt Ruby was the person of interest for the reporters.

'I'm keeping this chair for Steve,' she whispered, rolling up her jacket and placing it on the seat. 'I'd have thought he'd have been here by now! I hope nothing's wrong. That old clunker of his tends to break down at the most inconvenient moments.'

'Sorry I'm late!' Alyssa did a double-take as a tall figure slid into the adjoining seat, handing over her jacket in one smooth movement. She felt her face flushing.

'Tom! What on earth are you doing here?'

'Shush! Tell you later. It looks like we're about to get started.'

Everyone rose as the magistrate entered. She was a smartly dressed woman, not the silver-haired man they had expected. She quickly disposed of a number of cases, making decisions in a brisk manner. A youth had set fire to rubbish in the hallway of a block of flats. Another was in breach of his probation conditions and was given thirty days in jail. Ruby listened, fascinated, as the manager of the local Wal-Mart store described how a woman had been caught in the act of leaving the premises staggering under the weight of a television set she hadn't paid for.

Alyssa wriggled in her seat, every nerve fibre aware of the man seated next to her. She was furious that he had come. Steven wouldn't know what hit him when she gave him the telling off he deserved, for surely he was behind this switch, because of some misguided attempt to get her back together with Tom! At the same time, it was comforting to have him here for her, if only to fend off the reporters who would swarm them later.

Ruby's turn came at last. She listened meekly while the magistrate addressed the courtroom, talking about the folly of citizens taking the law into their own hands. 'I have spoken to Mayor Brunhofer and he has graciously agreed to drop all charges against Mrs Watson, believing that she did not act against him maliciously. He was merely in the wrong place at the wrong time. Mrs Watson, I believe that you have agreed to replace the shirt in question?'

Ruby nodded. Alyssa crossed her fingers. 'You're off the hook,' she hissed. 'Don't put your foot in it now.'

Of course Ruby couldn't hear this, being on the other side of the room.

Alyssa did not resist when Tom reached over, taking her hand in his. 'Don't worry, it'll be okay,' he whispered, and somehow she knew that he wasn't just talking about Ruby's problems.

'You have an excellent record in this area, Mrs Watson,' the magistrate went on. 'I myself did not have the privilege of coming under your care as a child, but I understand that many of our finest citizens have cause to thank you for their success today. In fact, this court has received many letters and emails, testifying to your good character and public-spirited behaviour.'

Ruby fumbled in her pocket for a tissue. 'Please, Lord, don't let me blub in front of all these people!' she begged.

'So I am persuaded that you acted out of stress, following a series of accidents that have taken a toll on a woman of your age. Therefore I urge you to give up any further thoughts you may have of engaging in juvenile behaviour on the streets of your hometown. This case is dismissed. You are free to go.'

Cameras clicked as Ruby stood tall on the courthouse steps. Answering questions with great dignity and the occasional descent into humour, she managed to imply that she was not giving up her campaign. Her reign of terror on the streets of Beegrove might be over, but there were other, more legal, methods she could try.

'It seems I rushed up here for nothing,' Tom remarked. 'Steve seemed to think you need protecting, but from what I can see the old girl has everything wrapped up nicely. The battling granny, indeed!'

'I'm glad you're here, Tom,' Alyssa said suddenly, surprising herself. Where had that come from?

'Are you, sweetheart? I had to come, just in case you needed me. I'll always be here for you, Alyssa. You know that, don't you?'

Alyssa started to reply, but then she bit back the words. This could be their chance to begin again, and there was no point in letting bitterness seep in. Perhaps if he listened carefully to what she had to say, he might understand what she'd found so upsetting about his failure to confide in her. In turn she'd let him explain his side of the story. Both of them had already tried to get their point across, of course, but the truth had become obscured by the heat of their emotions.

'I think it's time to whisk Aunt Ruby away,' she decided. 'She may look as though she's having a ball, but I know she tires easily, and I don't want to see her collapse later on. We'll get her home and have lunch, and then we can talk while she has her afternoon nap. Is that okay with you?'

'Okay by me!' Tom said, sweeping her into a bear hug.

Ruby came up to them, beaming with delight. 'Did you see that man in the navy blue suit? He's the school inspector for the region. I've been invited to visit the schools to talk to children about showing respect for senior citizens.'

Tom pulled a face. 'I'm sure that will go down like a lead balloon,' he muttered.

'Not if I approach the subject in the right way,' Ruby told him. 'I'll take my pistol along and tell them how I shot the mayor. That should get their attention.'

'That's if it doesn't give them some new ideas of their own,' Alyssa said. 'Come on, Auntie. Time to go home for lunch.'

30

'This is nice!' Ruby said, smiling brightly as Alyssa set down a plate in front of her. The salad was a colourful mix of lettuce, cucumber, tomatoes, chopped celery, radishes, sliced red peppers and devilled eggs.

'It would have been better if I'd thought to stop at the deli for some cooked chicken,' Alyssa replied. 'A plateful of rabbit food doesn't make for much of a celebration. Why don't I make some toasted tomato sandwiches to go with this lot?'

'No, dear, I wasn't talking about the salad, although I'm sure I'll enjoy it. And yes, do make a sandwich for Tom. Men need more than a few lettuce leaves to keep them going. What I meant was, it's lovely to have us all here together, so I can get to know your Tom a little better. Now, what shall we talk about?'

'Your victory in court, perhaps?' Tom suggested.

'I think we've heard enough about that for one day,' Alyssa said. 'If you're really interested to know what Auntie has planned for the future of her save-the-world campaign, just read it in the papers tomorrow. They'll have it all down pat, I'm sure.'

He stared at her in surprise. 'Did someone get up on the wrong side of the bed this morning? I thought you'd be overjoyed that your aunt has escaped a prison sentence.'

'There was never any danger of that, as you must know very well. What a stupid thing to say!'

Ruby looked at her niece in alarm. 'We've all been under a strain lately. Let's change the subject, shall we? Now, Tom, I don't quite understand about this business of your sister turning up out of the blue as she did. Did you really have no idea of her existence before now?'

Really, Alyssa thought. *We might be back in the classroom, with Auntie calling on a pupil to give a book report! I hope Tom won't get all upset by this and hightail it back to Mississauga before we've had a chance to talk between ourselves.*

But Tom seemed happy to respond to Ruby, whose facial expression showed her loving concern. 'Well, she showed up at the college one morning, quite unannounced. I happened to have a spare period, so when they paged me from the front office I was able to see her at once. She struck me as being slightly familiar, but I thought she might be a former student dropping in to say hello when she was passing through the area. Students tend to do that occasionally, particularly if they've enjoyed the course I teach.'

'I know, dear. It happens all the time to me. And of course I remember all their little faces, even thirty years or so later.'

'I'm sure. Well, she introduced herself

as Dixie Paulsen, a name I'd never heard before. We chattered back and forth for a few minutes, getting nowhere, and then she suddenly blurted it out. 'I'm your sister. I've come all this way so we can meet.'

'You know what students are like. At first I thought it was some sort of joke, although I couldn't see the point of it. Then she went on to say that my name was really Paulsen, which was ridiculous.' Tom stared into the distance, remembering the scene. 'I said, 'I'm sorry, Ms Paulsen. You've somehow got hold of the wrong fellow. My name is definitely Carson. My parents are dead now, killed in a car smash, but I was the only son of Robert and Maura Carson of Sydney, Nova Scotia.'

''I guess they adopted you, then. When my Mom was dying she told me about you. She wanted me to come and find you, so I wouldn't be alone in the world. My dad — our dad, that is — was Andrew Paulsen. He took off when I was little. Mom thought he was dead, but we could never be sure. Anyway, according to her, he always said he had a kid back East, and that would be you, Tom.'

''Do you have any proof of this fantastic story, Ms Paulsen?'

''Dixie, please. Not exactly, but why would Mom lie?'

''I can think of a number of reasons,' I said grimly.

'She said that letters used to come from some woman back East, who signed herself M. Carson, saying she needed money to buy things for little Tommy. 'Mom figured it was an old girlfriend, or maybe the mother of some girl he'd got into trouble.'

''But didn't she ask your father to explain?'

'Dixie shrugged. 'When he got drinking the only explaining he'd do was a thump on the head. I guess Mom wanted a quiet life, so she had to let it go.'

'I thought about this. 'How did you find me, Dixie?'

''It wasn't hard. Mom seemed to

recall that the Carson letters came from Sydney, so I trawled the internet for Carsons and came up with you. Your bio names you as the son of the late Robert John Carson of Sydney.'

''Coincidence!' I snapped, cursing the internet. It certainly has its uses, but at the same time it strips a person of all privacy. I looked sternly at the petite girl and said, 'I'm sorry; I just don't buy any of this. It's way too thin a story. For all I know this is some kind of scam. I have no idea what you hope to get out of this, but I'm not about to fall for it. Now, if that's all, I have classes to prepare for, so I must ask you to leave.'

'Tears welled up in the girl's myopic brown eyes. 'But you're all I have in the world, Tom! Please don't send me away! I've come so far to find you. You've got to give me a chance!''

* * *

He hesitated. 'And that's where I made my mistake,' he said, biting his lip as he looked at Ruby's eager expression. 'I thought: what if it's true? What if I really do have a young sister? Can I live with myself if I send her away to fend for herself? And what about me? I'd be wondering about all this for the rest of my life. If I didn't manage to get to the bottom of it, it would drive me crazy in the end.'

'Quite a dilemma, for sure,' Ruby agreed. 'But why not tell Alyssa about this?'

'That's exactly what I said!' Alyssa grumbled.

Ruby held up a warning finger. 'Let the boy continue, dear. Your turn will come later.'

'It's hard to explain, Mrs Watson. If Dixie's story was true, it wiped out all my preconceived notions about who I was and where I came from. Had my mother given birth to me out of wedlock? Had she had an affair with this Paulsen guy? Had the Carsons come by me because I was given up for adoption by some unknown girl? What if that adoption hadn't been legal? I was completely thrown by this. I didn't even want to think about the possibilities for a while, let alone talk about them.'

'This is all a lot of nonsense!' Alyssa interrupted. 'As I said at the time, what does it matter if you were adopted? It doesn't change who you are! Thousands of people are adopted and they don't get all bent out of shape because of it.'

Ruby frowned. 'If I may say so, dear, you're being particularly obtuse. You speak from the position of one who hasn't shared that experience. You were born to Greg and Anna, and I know that for a fact. You spent your growing-up years in a secure home and family, never having to doubt who you were. Why,' she added, warming to her theme, 'by what I've read in magazines, adopted children have many concerns in later life, no matter how loving and secure their childhood was. Who were my birth parents? Why did my mother give me up? Didn't she want me? Where is she now? Are there medical problems in my background that I should know about?'

Alyssa nodded slowly. Instead of trying to understand, she'd been harping on about Tom's failure to confide in her. And he hadn't simply been worrying about his own feelings. The situation had raised doubts in his mind about his beloved mother. Of course he had wanted to learn the truth about that before committing himself to their future together. And it was she, Alyssa, who had thrown back her ring in a fit of the pique.

'I'm sorry,' she whispered. 'I shouldn't have been so quick off the mark.'

Ruby nodded approvingly as Tom reached over to take Alyssa's hand in his.

'I'm sure I should have felt the same if my Philip had been seen squiring another girl around town on the eve of our marriage!' Ruby said. 'And I can't say I blame Steven for mentioning the fact. No doubt he was only trying to protect you.'

'I know how it must have looked,' Tom said miserably, 'but at the time I couldn't see anything wrong with it, considering the fact that she is my sister. If I could turn back the clock and do things differently, I would, but at the time I hardly knew which way to jump. Nothing seemed real to me any more, not even what we had together, Alyssa. I'm so sorry, but that's the way it was.'

The doorbell rang, making all three of them jump. Alyssa answered the door to the Presbyterian minister and the whole atmosphere changed.

'I just stopped by to see how you're faring after your ordeal,' the young clergyman said, grinning. 'I suppose you put them all to rout, as usual, Mrs Watson?'

'I'm not so sure about that, Mr Renison, but at least I was let off with a caution and told to come home and behave myself.'

'And will you manage that, do you think?'

Ruby's chin came up. 'It's hard to

say. The leopard doesn't change his spots overnight.'

'If at all,' Tom whispered, nudging Alyssa.

'What was that, Tom? Oh, I haven't introduced you, Reverend. You've met Alyssa, of course, and this is her young man, Tom Carson, from Mississauga.'

After greetings had been exchanged the minister left, refusing a cup of tea on the grounds that he had a lot of calls to make that afternoon. Tom disappeared into the bathroom, and Alyssa went upstairs to find her sneakers, because her feet were killing her in her smart three-inch heels. Any further discussion of Tom's misdoings would have to wait.

31

Negotiations were resumed over a delicious meal that Tom had brought in from Wendy's. The two women had ordered the chain's popular grilled chicken sandwiches, passing up one of their delicious salads on the grounds that they'd been virtuous earlier in the day and didn't need to go overboard. Tom had treated himself to two large burgers with cheese and bacon and a large helping of fries. Alyssa decided that this wasn't the moment to lecture him on healthy eating, especially as he might have chosen poutine, a recipe originating in Quebec that was a glorious mixture of fries, cheese curds and gravy that Wendy's now sold.

She was now aware of what Ruby was up to: expertly trying to help them sort out their problems. There was no telling where this might lead, but surely an exploration of the facts could do no harm.

'Perhaps you should explain to us now how you came to be staying in Dixie's flat,' Ruby said, licking her fingers as she swallowed the last morsel of chicken. 'I'm sure that Alyssa has been concerned about that little piece of the puzzle.'

Tom glanced at Alyssa and sighed. 'Looking back on it, I think I must have been mad,' he admitted. 'First of all, I want to assure you that Dixie is no longer in the picture. I've finally seen her for what she is, but more on that in a minute. After we broke up I had nowhere to go because I'd let my lease run out, expecting to be off to Australia. I didn't really want to mooch off friends, so when Dixie suggested I move into her rented place I saw no harm in it. She is my sister, after all.'

'And are you sure of that?' Ruby demanded.

'Oh, yes. Well, that is, I believe I'm the son of Andrew Paulsen, and she is his daughter, so . . . '

'Really!'

'Well, the elderly lady I spoke to at Rosebank seemed to know all about the man, and why should she lie? He and my mother were married, I was born and my birth father took off for points West. That much is clear to me now. Then, according to Dixie, he married or had a relationship with her mother and Dixie entered the equation.'

'Well, lots of marriages break up, for whatever reason. And where is your birth father now?'

Tom shrugged. 'Dixie doesn't seem to know whether he's dead or alive.'

'A rather unsatisfactory character, wouldn't you say?'

'The girl seems to have inherited those genes,' Alyssa said. 'She sounds a bit helpless and hopeless to me. From what you say she doesn't want to work and she's not interested in training for anything useful, either.'

'I agree,' Ruby said. 'I thought that the idea of relying on a man to keep one went out with the ark. Doesn't she have any pride? She'll have to pull up her socks before long if she hopes to get on in the world, and if you cave in to her, Tom, you'll have her hanging around your neck like an albatross!'

Tom scratched his neck, which had suddenly begun to itch. 'I've already seen that for myself, Mrs Watson. She has an uncle with her now — or perhaps it's a cousin; I'm not sure. And now I know that she's not alone in the world I can move on with a quiet conscience.' He turned to Alyssa. 'So now that Dixie is no longer a threat, where does that leave us? Am I forgiven for getting involved with her?'

Alyssa stared at him. 'I was never against your getting involved with her, as you put it. After the initial shock of learning that you had a sibling, of course you'd want to get to know her. And when you saw that she needed help, it was natural that you'd want to be there for her — although not, I might add, to the extent of bringing her into our home as a sort of third party to our marriage.'

'Well, there's no thought of that now, so are we all right? Is our engagement on again?'

'Oh, I'm not saying that,' Alyssa said. 'As I keep trying to tell you, this is all a matter of trust.' She stood up suddenly. 'I'm sorry. I've had all I can take for the moment. I'm going to have a bath, if that's all right with you, Auntie.'

'Certainly, dear. There should be plenty of hot water. We've all had a stressful day and it's time to relax. Off you go. I'll keep this young man entertained.'

Unable to follow, Tom fidgeted in his seat, resting his elbows on his knees. 'That's the end of that, then,' he muttered.

Ruby leaned forward to pat him on the hand. 'You mustn't give in to despair, dear. I'm sure that Alyssa still loves you. She needs time to come to terms with everything you've told her.'

'Time is just what we haven't got,

Mrs Watson. I can't just sit around doing nothing, while I wait for her to come to her senses. I've no job and no home. If there's no future for us I'll have to get my act together, very soon.'

Ruby put on her stern schoolteacher expression and prepared to rush in where angels fear to tread. 'Tom, just think about what you've just said! You expect that poor girl to come to her senses, as you put it! Isn't it time you did the very same thing? Yes, you've both made mistakes, but they are not so bad that the situation can't be mended. Forget about who is right and who is wrong and start *caring*. Let Alyssa see that you love her and have her best interests at heart. You seem to have gone overboard with caring about Dixie Paulsen; doesn't your future wife deserve as much, and more?'

'I don't know what else to do,' he replied.

'Think back to the time when you first discovered your love for each other,' Ruby suggested. 'Remember the days when your time spent together seemed all too short; when all you wanted was to please each other, and hoped for all good things for the other person. I may sound old-fashioned, but you must woo the girl. Make her believe that in your eyes she's the most important person in the world. Bring her flowers. Take her to restaurants and dine by candlelight. Take walks in the park. Oh, I don't know! Just use your imagination, man!'

'I suppose I could try,' he said.

Ruby clicked her teeth in exasperation. 'There's no 'suppose' about it! I have a feeling that this is your last chance, Tom Carson. Either you take it or you lose that girl forever. If that happens, don't say I didn't warn you!' She suddenly felt very tired. 'I'm sorry, young man; I think I'll have to go and lie down. My court appearance has taken more out of me than I thought. Now, you won't run off if I leave you alone, will you? I want to see you making a good start on the road to reconciliation.'

'I promise I'll stay, Mrs Watson.' Left alone in the kitchen, Tom gazed out of the window at his car, parked on the side of the street. It would be so easy to leave, clinging to his hurt feelings. He loved Alyssa with all his heart but he didn't know how to reach her.

Robert Carson, the man he thought of as his real father, had been a quiet, undemonstrative man, while his mother had been a traditional housewife, deferring to her husband in most ways. Perhaps she'd opted for a quiet life after what must have been a rocky road, married to Andrew Paulsen.

Alyssa was totally different: a thoroughly modern woman. She was bright, hard-working and willing and able to stand up for herself. He would not have wanted her to be any other way. This, after all, was the woman he'd fallen in love with. He, on the other hand, was unable to express his feelings. He was afraid to make a fool of himself. Afraid of rejection, he thought.

Alyssa came into the room, fresh from her bath. She was wearing a faded blue terrycloth robe and her dampened hair was pinned up on top of her head.

'You look adorable,' Tom blurted.

She laughed. 'What brought that on?'

'If you only knew how much I love you, you wouldn't have to ask that,' he continued, surprising himself. 'Come back to me, my darling. Please, please come back to me. I don't want to live without you!'

'What will you do if I refuse, Tom Carson?'

'Why, then I'll follow you to Australia. I'll follow you to the ends of the earth, if that's what it takes.'

'Stalking me, huh? I'll have you know I'm friends with a very nice policeman who'll put you in your place if I ask him.' Seeing his wounded expression, she decided to put him out of his misery.

'Okay, okay! I'm only joking. Of course I'll come back to you, Tom Carson. I've missed you. But get this.

You'd better not find any more missing siblings, or I might change my mind!'

'From what I know of Andrew Paulsen, anything is possible. But if anything like that does crop up, we'll deal with it together. I've learned my lesson, teacher.' He swept her into his arms then, giving her a sweet, lingering kiss. This she returned with good measure.

Releasing her with a sigh, Tom took a step back, fumbling in the inside pocket of his tweed jacket. 'I guess you'll be needing this,' he said, producing a tiny enamelled pillbox, which he opened to reveal her ring, nestling in a puff of cotton wool.

'You've been carrying that around with you all this time?' Alyssa marvelled, holding out her left hand for the return of the jewel that was the pledge of their love. Suddenly the mists that had obscured her deep love for this man melted away. It seemed to her as if this ordinary little room was lit up by a thousand stars as they kissed once more.

Engrossed in the beauty of the moment they failed to hear Aunt Ruby, who had come padding downstairs in search of a cup of tea. She stood in the doorway, beaming with joy.

'Well now,' she whispered, 'will you just look at that! It seems to me that everything is about to come right for my two turtle doves, and I'm happy to think that I may have played a part in that!'

So Alyssa and Tom had taken the first steps back onto the path that beckoned them into the future. They were all set to make a new life together, with love from Aunt Ruby.

THE END

We do hope that you have enjoyed reading this large print book.

Did you know that all of our titles are available for purchase?

We publish a wide range of high quality large print books including:
Romances, Mysteries, Classics
General Fiction
Non Fiction and Westerns

Special interest titles available in large print are:
The Little Oxford Dictionary
Music Book, Song Book
Hymn Book, Service Book

Also available from us courtesy of Oxford University Press:
Young Readers' Dictionary
(large print edition)
Young Readers' Thesaurus
(large print edition)

Other titles in the
Linford Romance Library:

MORE THAN A PORTRAIT

Diana Dennison

When Jane is offered a job in northern Italy, with its promise of sunshine and colour, mountains and romantic scenery, her adventurous spirit can hardly refuse. Then she meets her employer: the unpredictable, pompous and dictatorial Duncan Frobisher. Sparks immediately fly between them, and Jane comes to know more than her fair share of elation and black depression before her temporary employment comes to an end . . .

FORGOTTEN

Fay Cunningham

Driving home in the dark, Serena stops to help an injured man lying in a ditch. He mutters something unintelligible, but that is only the start of her problems. Someone is watching the apartment she shares with her brother, her mother is being particularly secretive, and police detective Jack Armstrong is convinced Serena is hiding something. Just when she thinks things can get no worse, her missing father turns up. This is definitely not the time to fall in love.

A PERFECT RHAPSODY

Dawn Bridge

After an unhappy romance with a concert pianist, Emma joins her local orchestra — something she has always wanted to do. Their new young conductor, Paul, seems to be an aloof and arrogant man, but Emma finds herself attracted to him. What secret is he concealing? Will she be able to break through the barrier which he has erected around himself? And how can she ever hope to compete with the beautiful Samantha for his affections, whilst dealing with admirers of her own?

TIDES OF LOVE

Phyllis Mallett

When her widowed father dies, Clarissa Marston is left penniless. George Farand, however, has a solution: in debt to the late Mr. Marston, he invites Clarissa to stay with his family at their Cornish estate of Trevarron until he can repay her the money. She warms to the genial John Farand, despite his darkly brooding brother Edwin. But Trevarron is a place of ominous secrets, and Clarissa begins to fear for her safety — until the handsome Richard Redmond comes to her aid . . .

FATE IN FREEFALL

Ken Preston

Paralysed by grief after losing her fiancé in a skydiving accident, Katrina Maslow cannot allow herself to love another man. She travels the world in an attempt to flee from her former life, ending up in Rio and accepting a job as a guide with J Stone Adventure Trips. But Jay, the handsome owner of the company, is determined to break down her reserves. As they are pursued by a ruthless killer, Katrina finally realises she is in love with Jay — just at the moment she might lose him forever . . .

THE TIGER IN MEN

Denise Robins

When Fenella Shaw left England to take possession of a Canadian cattle ranch in the Saskatchewan Valley, gifted to her as a legacy by her father, she quickly fell in love with handsome Max Geerling, the manager. It came as no surprise to anyone when the news of their engagement was announced, the neighbouring farmers believing them to be ideally matched. But Max is not all he seems to be — and Fenella finds herself caught up in a situation so alien to her that she fears she may never escape . . .